For Dev.

The Ring of Kerry Hannigan

A NOVELLA

CIJI WARE

Poggio's is "mentioned in dispatches" in this story

With Thanks
Ciji

aug. 2015

Cover design 2015 by The Killion Group, Inc.
http://thekilliongroupinc.com/
Cover and colophon design by Kim Killion.
http://www.hotdamndesigns.com/
Photo credit of Chaffin Orchards olive grove: Anthony Dunn
http://www.adunnphotography.com/
Formatting & copyediting A Thirsty Mind Book Design
http://www.athirstymind.com/

ISBN: 978-0-9889408-9-5

Additional Library of Congress Cataloging-in-Publication Data available upon request.

1. 21st Century Women's fiction.
2. Romantic fiction.
3. Culinary arts.
4. American chefs.
5. Women chefs.
6. Food blogging.
7. Olive oil.
8. American olive oil production.
9. Internet start-ups.
10. Magical realism.

THE RING OF KERRY HANNIGAN is published by Lion's Paw Publishing, a division of Life Events Media LLC, 1001 Bridgeway, Ste. J-224, Sausalito, CA 94965.

For information contact: www.cijiware.com

This novella is dedicated to

My treasured friends of long-standing, Diane Barr, Susan Wintersteen, Terry Cagney Morrison, and Diane Worthington

Praise for Ciji Ware's

THE RING OF KERRY HANNIGAN

"...Oozing magic and romance. I'm not even Irish and I loved it."
– BARBARA FREETHY, #1 *New York Times* bestselling author of *That Summer Night*

"This will leave your heart in San Francisco in ways you never imagined. Brava!"
– MARY ALICE MONROE, *New York Times* bestselling author of *The Summer Wind*

"Ingenious, entertaining and utterly romantic...A terrific read."
– JANE HELLER, *New York Times* and *USA Today* bestselling author

"I read straight through..."
– MARY JO PUTNEY, *New York Times* bestselling author of *Sometimes a Rogue*

Praise for Ciji Ware's
Contemporary and Historical Fiction

"A fascinating portrayal…with characters convincingly drawn…Ware again proves she can intertwine fact and fiction to create an entertaining and harmonious whole."
– PUBLISHERS WEEKLY

"…Fiction at its finest…beautifully written."
– LIBBY'S LIBRARY NEWS

"A mesmerizing blend of sizzling romance…love and honor…Ciji Ware has written an unforgettable tale."
– THE BURTON REVIEW

"A novel so lively and intriguing, you don't realize you've learned anything till after you close the book. Exciting, entertaining, and enlightening."
– LITERARY TIMES

"…A story so fascinating that it should come with a warning—do not start unless you want to be up all night!"
– ROMANTIC TIMES

"A well-researched and entertaining novel…excellent."
– LIBRARY JOURNAL

"Ciji Ware has created a gorgeous tapestry…A deep, complex novel exploring love, betrayal, healing, and renewal in the human heart."
– AFFAIRE DE COEUR

Titles by Ciji Ware

Historical Novels

Island of the Swans
Wicked Company
A Race to Splendor

"Time-Slip" Historical Novels

A Cottage by the Sea
Midnight on Julia Street
A Light on the Veranda

Contemporary Novels

The Four Seasons Quartet:
That Summer in Cornwall
That Autumn in Edinburgh
That Winter in Venice – coming 2015
That Spring in Paris – coming 2016

Contemporary Novellas

Ring of Truth: "The Ring of Kerry Hannigan"

Nonfiction

Rightsizing Your Life
Joint Custody After Divorce

When your heart speaks...will you listen?

On the eve of a move from New York to San Francisco, classically trained chef and respected food blogger Kerry Hannigan's world turns upside down the instant she puts on an Irish Claddagh ring—the timeless Irish symbol of love, friendship and fidelity worn not only by Jackie Kennedy and Princess Grace, but by scores of citizens and firefighters who fought their last battle in New York's Twin Towers on 9/11.

A gift from her godmother, the emerald gemstone reputedly offers life-changing guidance and counsel—but only for seven days, and only to those who *listen.*

Is it serendipity—or something else—when Kerry lands her dream job among groves of the Montisi Olive Ranch in beautiful Sonoma, north of San Francisco? And is one week long enough to know if Renato Montisi is all he appears to be, or just another "player" like the man she left behind?

Chapter One

The cab door nearly blew off its hinges when its harried passenger prepared to step out of the taxi and on to the curb at 83rd and Park Avenue on a blustery, rain-soaked December afternoon. Kerry Hannigan was late by nearly a half-hour and feared she was about to disappoint her favorite person in the world—again.

Drenched by the downpour in the time it took her to sprint to the front door of her godmother's co-op building, the thirty-three-year-old nodded politely to the uniformed doorman who ushered her across the hushed lobby's black-and-white marble squares leading toward the familiar set of brass-trimmed elevators. She'd been riding up to the fourteenth floor ever since the day her mother and grandmother selected Angelica Fabrini Doyle to serve as Kerry's legal guardian, should anything happen to her parents. Their choice for the only Hannigan daughter had occurred long after their beloved friend had met and happily married their cousin Brian Doyle, a successful corporate lawyer who had not only shocked his Irish friends and colleagues "by marrying Italian," but had also changed the former seamstress's life forever.

As the elevator lifted smoothly toward the higher floors, Kerry could almost hear her godmother repeat a mantra she had lived by all her life: "'Friendship, loyalty, and love,' Kerry, my pet. That's what my darling Brian taught me about being happy. If you have that, you have all of life's riches!"

Oh, how she would miss Angelica's wisdom and the love this woman had lavished on her since birth! She dreaded the moment when she had to explain to the octogenarian how long she would be away from New York, but there was no avoiding a full disclosure this afternoon about what was happening in her life—and that moment was *now*.

The elevator doors slid open and Kerry padded toward Number 3 at the end of the hall where her godmother's four-bedroom palace overlooked Park Avenue. Her late godfather had not only been a loving, sweetheart of a guy, recalled Kerry fondly, but he had managed to be both hugely successful *and* ethical, representing wealthy clients suing certain wayward money managers for fraud.

Even so, her godparents' lives had not *all* been a perfect fantasy, had it, she reflected? Kerry tried not to let thoughts of Maggie Doyle add to the jumble of emotionally-charged issues she had already been wrestling with from the moment Charlie excitedly burst into her office cubicle with his big announcement, "Pack your bags, kiddo…you're gonna be a millionaire!"

She drew closer to Angelica's front door at the end of the hallway, hoping that her boots weren't leaving discernible puddles on the expensive carpeting. She paused, inhaled a deep breath, and pushed the buzzer. Within seconds, she heard footsteps and the door to the Doyle's abode swung open.

"Kerry, pet!" Angelica held her arms wide and then noted how soaked from the rain her visitor was. "Oh, my goodness! Look at you, you poor dear! I'll hug you in a minute. Come in, come in, and let's get you out of that dripping raincoat! Molly's got the tea brewing for us in the living room."

Kerry couldn't help but feel her spirits lift as the sprightly, ageless Angelica, stylish as ever in pleated grey wool trousers and a matching grey cashmere sweater set, hung up her visitor's coat in the hall closet, chaffed her goddaughter's cold hands, and led her briskly into the elegantly appointed front room that almost seemed like a movie set.

Kerry's glance absorbed the well-remembered peach-colored, Thai silk matching sofas and Louis XIV chairs gathered around a glowing fireplace whose ornate marble mantel was graced with a ceiling-high, gilt-framed mirror reflecting back the beauty of the entire chamber.

Angelica patted the sofa cushion next to her to indicate her godchild should sit down beside her.

"I'll take things from here, thank you, Molly, dear," she bid her maid of many years. Angelica turned to her goddaughter. "Even though it's nearly five o'clock, you prefer good, strong, Irish Breakfast tea with a little milk, if I remember, yes, Kerry?"

"Yes please, and I'm so sorry I was late," Kerry replied, hoping she didn't sound too defensive. "The crosstown traffic—"

"The point is you're here, now, and that's all that matters."

Kerry adored her godmother, but lately, there had been long periods between their visits and she'd missed sharing confidences with Angelica in ways she'd never been able to do with her busy, preoccupied parents. As long as she could remember, she'd basked in the warm glow of affection that she'd always felt whenever they were together. Charlie never seemed to understand how indebted she felt to the older woman for having gifted her with a very expensive certificated course at the Culinary Institute of America in Hyde Park, outside New York City. When Kerry had protested the $53,000 price tag for the program, her godmother had scoffed.

"It's the Harvard of cooking schools, for pity's sake, and you are far more the chef than your mother or father ever were! I merely want to offer you an alternative to life at Hannigan's Bar and Grill!" she'd teased the year Kerry was poised to enter her sixth season as sous chef to her mother since graduating from a local community college. "This degree will be your ticket to working in the finest restaurants anywhere…and maybe even to opening one of your own someday. There are lots of successful female chefs nowadays, my dear…and I think *you* could be one of them!"

And yet what did I do *with all that knowledge. . . .?*

In her mind's eye, a cascading image of endless late nights at her desk in the CookChic.com's office in Brooklyn flashed before her. During the two years since she'd graduated from the CIA, she had slaved away in her tiny, three-sided cubicle creating new, up-to-the-minute blog posts about New York's culinary scene. As for cooking itself, she hadn't tried anything new or ambitious in months, and—

Her guilty thoughts were interrupted by her godmother handing her a steaming cup of tea in eggshell-thin, Irish Belleek chinaware that had belonged to Brian Doyle's late mother.

"So tell me, Kerry, dear," her godmother said, forcing the younger woman's thoughts back to the present, "I want to hear all about the new development you mentioned on the phone. You hinted it might involve spending some time in California? It's all happened so quickly."

Kerry explained in as little detail as possible that Charlie Miller, her classmate at the legendary culinary academy, had helped her launch a food blog for the serious home chef who occasionally likes to dine out.

"Charlie knew how to drive tons of traffic to my blog because he is, as he calls himself, 'King of the Key Words'— thanks to a series of tech jobs he had before he enrolled in the CIA."

"That can't be the only reason your blog has been so successful," Angelica protested.

Her godmother's staunch loyalty brought a grateful smile to Kerry's lips.

"Well, his knowledge of how social media works, combined with a pretty great recipe of mine at the end of every post, apparently made a good combination," she allowed. "We formed a fifty-fifty partnership in our little start-up business, and suddenly, we were getting thousands and thousands of hits and—"

"Hits? That doesn't sound good," Angelica interrupted.

"In the Internet world, hits are a *very* good thing," Kerry assured her. "In fact, the number of daily visitors to our site got so impressive that a company called LifestyleXer in San Francisco made an offer for us to become part of a bigger site that provides my age group everything from online apartment listings to home furnishing tips to…well…guidance and recipes from me for the busy home chef, along with my recommendations about the best places to dine out when amateur cooks don't feel like cooking."

"Well, how exciting, dear," Angelica complimented her mildly.

"Yes, it is…and now, as part of this bigger company, I'll be expanding to *two* blogs a day, Monday through Friday. The new company also wants us to find and manage other bloggers in ten major cities around the country, based on my template."

"That sounds like quite an additional challenge," Angelica commented, regarding Kerry closely.

"Our deal with them, though," Kerry replied, not meeting her godmother's steady gaze because this was going to be the hard part of what she had to tell her Angelica today, "is that we have work in San Francisco. Starting tomorrow."

There! She'd finally said the words: she was moving away…

"But it's three weeks before Christmas!" Angelica protested.

"I know...I tried to get that changed, but...they said no."

Angelica remained silent and then took a slow, measured sip of her tea. Finally she said, "And has the company that bought yours at least made it financially worth to go through such a rather major upheaval in your life?"

It was Kerry's turn to stare into the milky depths of her teacup.

"Well...we're considered a start-up division within LifestyleXer, so we'll still be earning a modest salary, *but,*" she emphasized with all the enthusiasm she could muster, "the company is paying for our move and Charlie and I are due half a million dollars, each, in vested stock options, at the end of two years—"

"Two *years*!"

Kerry could understand how—for an eighty-one-year-old—the thought of far fewer visits and coping with different time zones was...well...unsettling.

"Two years," she repeated, "if the IPO goes through this January."

"The IPO?" Angelica echoed. "Your new company is going to make an Initial Public Offering of its stock?"

Angelica Doyle read *The Wall Street Journal* religiously and was certainly no neophyte in business.

"Yes. The San Francisco dot com is going to offer its stock to the public in a few weeks," she disclosed. "And we'll be granted *more* shares, down the road, if the food blogging part of the business continues to do well after the two years."

"Hmmm, stock *options*," mused her godmother. "So your pay-out as a result of this move is not a sure thing?"

Angelica Doyle had been the consummate businesswoman in the interior design firm she had founded and run for many decades and was no pushover, as Kerry could plainly see.

"It's a fairly sure thing, as these things go," she replied carefully. "The IPO is all teed up for the first of the year, so once that happens, all we have to do is wait for our stock to vest and then sell it in batches of twenty-five percent a fiscal quarter after that two-year date."

"*If* the stock price retains its value all that time, yes?" Angelica pressed. "Sometimes these ventures don't, you know."

"Charlie thinks that LifestyleXer might be another LinkedIn."

The tiniest frown had appeared between Angelica's eyebrows.

"I take it that meanwhile, *you're* the one busy writing all those blogs and managing the compatriots you find and hire?"

"Well…right."

"And will you do any hands-on culinary work for your new employer?"

"Well, no…but—"

"And what is your…business partner, Mr. Miller, going to be doing during the two-year waiting period?"

Kerry could tell that Angelica couldn't quite bring herself to call Charlie Miller her godchild's "boyfriend" or even her "beau." Kerry had never described to her godmother the way in which Charlie had swept her off her feet from the first day of class with adulation both for her person and her cooking. And despite the fact that Kerry and Charlie had lived together for nearly a year, Angelica had met him only once on an occasion when Charlie's one-syllable answers to her godmother's polite attempts to draw him out had been less than inspiring for either of them. Angelica was a wildly creative, visually oriented person. Kerry wasn't surprised her godmother couldn't appreciate a tech-focused guy like Charlie, and she felt impelled to defend him.

"Oh, he'll share his Internet expertise with the larger company and will still be pushing traffic to my blog and the other ones we're going to establish around the country," she assured her with a bright smile. "Charlie's work should make the stock even more attractive to potential investors."

"I see…" murmured Angelica. "So that's why the move to San Francisco. And what about any face-to-face connecting for you with experts in the food world out west? Will you have time to do some of that?"

Angelica's probing questions hung in the air several moments before Kerry answered.

"Well, I'll certainly be interviewing those sorts of people on the phone for my blog, and as far as cooking, we've been so busy, we usually eat out. For research."

Her godmother paused and then asked pointedly, "And is this move what *you* want to do?"

Kerry hesitated, and then replied, "As you just said, it's all happened so fast, Angelica. The sudden sale of CookChic…and then, as part of the deal, the west coast execs subsequently insisted that we move to San Francisco to be close to headquarters. But it's only for two years—" she reiterated.

"It's been two *years* since you got your degree from the CIA, pet," Angelica reminded her quietly—as if she needed to.

Kerry felt a rush of warmth invade her fair skin and she wondered, suddenly, if her black hair and blue eyes conjured up for her wise, perceptive godmother a vision of an embarrassed Irish Snow White, indeed, mortified that she hadn't put her acknowledged culinary talents and training to practical use in the real world of top-flight food production, which was, after all, her true passion. She leaned forward and put her hand on the older woman's sleeve.

"Angelica, I will never be able to thank you enough for

paying my tuition at—"

"Kerry!" she interrupted in the sharpest tone of voice Kerry had ever heard her use. "That is not *at all* what I'm talking about here! Just as I did with my darling Maggie," she continued, referring to her late daughter, "I will always support you in whatever path you wish to follow. It's just I would hope it is *your* path. Not one that someone else has chosen *for* you."

Before Kerry could reply, her godmother thrust her hand between the sofa's silk cushions and withdrew a scuffed, burgundy leather ring box.

"The other reason that I asked you to come here—besides wanting to see you—is that I have a present for you. I suupose, now, we can call it an early Christmas gift."

"Oh, Angelica…you've given me so much and—"

"I gave this to Maggie back when she was a bit older than you are now. I will try once more to pass this on as it was passed to me."

Kerry stared, dumbfounded, as Angelica opened the leather box in whose depth was nestled a ring every self-respecting Irish-American would instantly recognize. She remembered that Maggie Doyle had worn the gold Claddagh ring every day since her mother had given it to her. How in the world did Angelica have it in her possession *now*…after…

From the small leather box, her godmother gently lifted the ring featuring two cupped, gold hands embracing an emerald gemstone cut in the shape of a heart and topped with a tiny, golden crown.

"You know," Angelica said softly, "the New York City police chief told me that one in five people who died in the Twin Towers on September Eleventh was of Irish extraction." She gazed somberly at the beautiful ring. "The numbers vary, depending on who you talk to, but twenty-three members of the NYPD, along with three hundred-plus firemen, and more than *six hundred* employees of the

Cantor Fitzgerald firm died that day. Many who worked there were Irish-Americans, like Maggie. When the recovery teams finally finished going through those acres of rubble, more than two hundred Claddagh rings similar to this one were found…"

"No!" exclaimed Kerry, stunned by this revelation.

"Well, I suppose it's not too surprising, since these rings are traditionally exchanged at Irish weddings and given as tokens of kinship and friendship."

Kerry's throat began to close and she could see tears edging into the corner of her godmother's eyes as well. It had been more than a decade since Maggie went off to work that sparkling Tuesday morning, a member of the legal staff at a prosperous bond brokerage house. Despite the young woman's earlier leanings toward a career in clothing design, she'd ultimately chosen law school, dark pinstripe business suits, and a penchant for "Ice Men"—as her mother once described the males that her daughter had occasionally brought home to dinner.

"I gave the ring to Maggie for her thirty-seventh birthday when she told me they were going to promote her to the top job in the legal department at work. I thought, perhaps, if she took advantage of the ring's…rather unusual powers, she might change the way her life was—"

"What do you mean 'unusual powers?'" Kerry interrupted, taken aback by what she'd thought she heard her godmother say.

"Maggie was conflicted," Angelica disclosed. "She wanted to please her father, even though he never urged her to follow in his footsteps. Brian was a wonderful husband, but his law practice demanded so much of his time that, looking back on it all, I think Maggie's going to law school instead of design school, and her taking that horrible grind-of-a-job in the Twin Towers, was just a way of asking for more of his attention."

"Oh, Angelica…" Kerry said, feeling tears about to

spill down her cheeks. "I can't imagine how hard it's been for you with both Maggie and Brian gone." She seized one of Angelica's hands. "And if *I've* disappointed you, I feel just horrible—"

"No!" Angelica said fiercely. "You haven't disappointed me one bit! I just don't want you to disappoint *yourself*! I want you to have this ring that was among those given back to the surviving relatives after that ghastly day. The victims' families were asked to list anything that might identify their loved ones, and one day I got a call and..."

Her godmother closed her eyes briefly and Kerry squeezed her hand, holding it tightly. Angelica bowed her head, and then continued to speak in a low voice.

"I can only assume that Maggie chose not to...to listen to what the ring had to teach her." She cast her goddaughter a piercing gaze. "Now, you can say I should be committed to a lunatic asylum if you want to, but you must trust me when I say *this* particular Claddagh ring can help you know what's truly in your heart!"

Kerry stared at the object in Angelica's hand, her godmother's aged fingers slightly swollen with arthritis.

"But *how*?" Kerry murmured, amazed to think the ring Maggie Doyle once wore had survived the devastation of that day and had eventually been returned to her mother. "How can a piece of jewelry—"

"*My* mother," Angelica began, "died years before you were born. She was a new Italian immigrant working at the Triangle Shirtwaist Factory in 1911. One of the young women who toiled beside her ten hours a day—an Irish girl—took Mama aside as they were walking home together late one night and gave her the ring, saying it had told *her* to quit her job that day and to pass the ring on to someone else who needed it."

"Oh, now, Angelica...how could—"

"Hear me out!" commanded her godmother. "The coworker told my mother that the ring had originally been made in the town of Claddagh on Galway Bay in Ireland. Mama swore to me that as soon as she put the ring on her finger, a voice in her head said to turn around and go home only a few minutes after she'd arrived at work at the shirt factory the next morning—which meant she was fired, of course."

"So what happened? Did the ring tell her where to find a better job?" Kerry teased.

Angelica shot her a stern look.

"That same day in March, 1911, the factory burned to the ground, killing 146 of the two girls' co-workers. Three days later, wandering into Hannigan's Bar and Grill—which was only a pub back then—Mama met your grandfather's cousin and married him." Angelica smiled faintly. "That man drinking Guinness that evening became my father."

"The ring *talks?*" Kerry asked, unable to keep the skepticism out of her tone.

"Not exactly. Not out loud. In my own case, I simply had *thoughts* surface in my mind. Thoughts that contained much wisdom, I might add."

"You're saying *you've* heard this ring silently speak to you?" Kerry queried. "Those were probably just your *own* thoughts!"

Angelica shrugged. "Maybe so, but the ring only spoke to me for one week. After that, the guidance ceased…but of course by then I'd met Brian Doyle."

Kerry couldn't refrain from teasing her once more. "Well how do you know it was the *ring* 'speaking?' From pictures I've seen of Brian in his youth, he was a pretty dishy guy. It wouldn't have taken anybody else to tell you that."

Angelica pointed to the heart-shaped emerald clasped between the ring's two golden hands.

"When certain thoughts popped into my head, the

emerald pulsed and turned opalescent…and when that happened, I knew it was the ring offering a message of guidance."

"Make it glow, then," demanded Kerry.

"Oh no, dear," protested Angelica, "I can't do that. As I say, its powers only last for seven days, starting from the moment a new wearer puts it on. That still, small voice of counsel and guidance is offered on a temporary basis only. The wearer can choose to follow the suggestions or not…and at the end of the week, the ring reverts to being simply a lovely piece of jewelry which one can wear as long as one likes until prompted to give it to another woman who needs it."

Kerry reached out and gently rested a finger on the emerald.

"Maggie was wearing this on September Eleventh? Why didn't it protect her, then?"

"Yes, she was wearing it. She loved the ring because it was beautiful and a gift from her father and me…but she told me flat out she thought the whole 'guidance thing' was ridiculous and a bunch of Irish hooey and she certainly didn't want to hear any advice to quit her job and go back to her first love—designing clothes."

"She told you the ring said to do that? To go back to the field of clothing design?"

"Whatever thoughts came into her head when she first put it on she just…ignored. Weeks went by. She was waiting for the retirement party of her mentor and the official announcement about her huge promotion. She was ambitious, you remember, which was *fine*, but I know she was lonely, which is why I had decided to pass on the ring to her that summer. Her job in those towers was all-consuming. She never seemed to have time for close relationships, except for those wolves of Wall Street she dated from time to time. She kept telling me 'I don't have the bandwidth to go out for lunch or drinks with people.'"

Angelica shook her head, murmuring almost to herself, "Imagine saying that about friends and family..."

A wall of misery Kerry had learned to keep mostly at bay was threatening, now, to engulf her godmother and her as they both fought off the terrible memories of those days following 9/11.

Desperate to guide the conversation in another direction, Kerry asked her, "So, what did the ring tell *you* to do when you were given it?"

"Me?" Angelica smiled at the memory, which was exactly what Kerry hoped would happen. "Back in those days, I was working two jobs to earn the money for interior design school...days doing clothing alterations at my parents' dry cleaners and nights at Hannigan's Bar and Grill on West 44th Street, smack in the middle of the theatre district. Your father, Patrick, was starting to take over the management—the fourth generation in the food business, you know, making *you* the fifth—" Angelica paused, and then amended, "Well, maybe not anymore..."

"Doesn't *writing* about food count?" Kerry demanded.

Angelica merely shrugged again.

"At any rate," her godmother continued, "one night, about two days after I'd been given the ring from my mother—who knew I wanted to be more than just a seamstress in a dry cleaner by day and a waitress by night—in walked Brian Doyle, dressed to the nines. That particular night, I had worn a lovely outfit that had been unclaimed at my parents' shop for a year and so I was put on duty up front, checking in the guests. The dapper Mr. Doyle had an extra ticket to a Broadway show and offered it to me as soon as he saw me there."

"What about your manning of the reservations desk?"

"I was quite shocked when a voice in my head said, '*Say yes to Mr. Doyle!*' so I ran to your Grandmother Hannigan, cooking in the back, and she made your father take over for me out front. From that moment on,"

Angelica added with a girlish giggle, "I listened carefully to every thought that came to me whenever the emerald turned into a glowing opal—even though most people I knew thought I was crazy, getting engaged in a month."

"Only a *month*?" Kerry replied, aghast.

"Actually, I accepted Brian's proposal on the seventh day I had the ring…we just didn't *tell* anyone for a month!"

Kerry laughed and shook her head. "Well, it was a love match, that's for sure." She glanced around the beautifully appointed living room, adding, "And look what a wonderful career you had."

"Brian made all that possible. Encouraged me to get the best training there was in interior design and bankrolled tuition at Parsons and my first few years in the business."

"But you barely *knew* the man when you married him!" Kerry protested. "Didn't you feel you were mighty lucky that it actually worked out? Who would have bet back then that you and Brian would turn out to be so well suited?"

"No, it wasn't luck!" her godmother replied emphatically. "We just *knew*." She glanced at the ornate clock on the mantel. "Well…it's getting late and I'm sure you have a million loose ends to tie up. I'm terribly sorry Mr. Miller couldn't come with you today, but…do give him my best."

Kerry had tried to persuade Charlie to join them for tea, but he'd begged off, as usual.

"Now put this in a safe place," Angelica said, securing the ring in its box and closing the lid. "You can choose to put it on whenever you like—or not at all. It's totally up to you, pet. Just remember, though, I give it to you with the greatest love."

Kerry's eyes grew moist again as she wrapped her arms around her godmother in a hug. Then, she slipped the ring box into the bottom of her handbag, wondering, suddenly, what her life would be like in California without Angelica close by? Her godmother was right to suspect that the new job might not allow the time to do more than search the Internet for artisan food entrepreneurs to interview by phone. Kerry had wondered lately if it was her destiny only to *read* about farm-to-table cuisine in Northern California—not experience it? Given her increased blogging schedule of two posts per day, and recruiting all those new writers, she seriously doubted she'd get to meet many of these food devotees in person. In fact, CookChic's only other female employee, Sally, had called their enterprise in Brooklyn "an electronic sweatshop." What would LifestyleXer prove to be?

Triangle Shirtwaist Factory indeed…

She glanced down at her purse and speculated about the choices she'd made since graduating from culinary school—and about a ring that could put thoughts in a person's head. By this time, she and Angelica had reached the apartment's front door and Kerry had donned her coat. Her godmother enfolded her in her arms one last time and then kissed her on both cheeks.

"Goodbye, Kerry, pet. I'll miss you *molto, molto.*"

"Goodbye, Angelica. I'll miss you, too. I love you," she added, as she had every time she'd said farewell to her godmother since the events of 9/11.

"I know that, darling girl, and it's been a great comfort, believe me."

A hollowness filled Kerry's chest. How long would it really be before she saw Angelica again? Her godmother had always been her rock, the person she could turn to. For months ahead, Kerry's work routine in San Francisco at the bigger company on the eve of an IPO would rule out even quick trips back to New York. As for speaking together on the phone, that three-hour time difference between coasts would be a killer. And how long, she wondered, would Angelica be as spry as she was these days?

The clock in the living room tolled the hour, its delicate brass pings reminding her that Charlie was probably waiting impatiently at their apartment for her to fix him something to eat.

Kerry summoned a cheery smile. "Now, don't forget to read your email!"

"No," her godmother said firmly. "Do the old fashioned thing and call me once in a while, will you? *Slàinte,*" she said, offering the Irish word for "To your health," instead of her usual "*Ciao, bellissima*!"

"*Ciao,* Angelica," Kerry replied, and walked swiftly down the hall as her godmother closed her front door.

The elevator swished to fetch her on the fourteenth floor, and in less than a minute whisked her down to the lobby where the doorman found her a cab for the ride across Manhattan in the pouring rain.

Chapter Two

By the time Kerry's cab pulled up in front of the apartment that she and Charlie Miller shared on 87th and West End Avenue, the rain had tapered off and her stomach was rumbling. She waited impatiently for the vintage elevator to arrive, wracking her brain about what to whip up for dinner.

Or maybe just send out for Thai…unless Charlie's already ordered in.

Hoping for the latter, she slipped her key into the lock and opened the front door. She gave a sniff, but detected no scent of dinner wafting from a bag of cardboard cartons waiting to be revived by the microwave in their minuscule kitchen.

"Hey, hi…I'm home!" she called. Her words had a hollow ring, now that the movers had loaded the van with their furniture.

Charlie's slender, brown-haired figure was hunched over his laptop sitting on a packing carton in the middle of their bare living room.

"Did you bring food home?" he said without looking up as he continued to type furiously.

"No, did *you?*" she retorted, annoyed it was always assumed *she* was responsible for putting food on the table every single night.

"You're an hour later than you said you'd be. I thought you must have stopped somewhere to get us something to eat."

"You were here all day," she protested. "Couldn't you

have run down to—"

"Cool it, Kerry," he snapped. "I had a few more pressing things than to drink tea on Park Avenue, you know what I'm saying?"

Stung, Kerry turned abruptly and marched into the four-foot-square kitchen and opened the refrigerator that barely came up to her waist. She proceeded to throw together two omelets with the four remaining eggs, a tired green onion, and a wilted half of a red pepper that she diced into tiny cubes with a vengeance. She dished this hurried fare onto the paper plates they'd been using since her dishes had been packed.

"Here you go," she announced, and left the food on a nearby suitcase they'd be taking with them in the morning.

She waited a millisecond for a "Thanks" and when it wasn't forthcoming, she headed directly for the bedroom. She ate her eggs while sitting on the bed that they'd previously sold to their neighbor who would move it across the hall once they'd left. In twenty-four hours, this room would be empty of any trace she'd ever lived here, and, for some reason, that thought brought a huge lump to her throat.

She rose to her feet, swiftly shed her clothes, and hopped into the shower, allowing a fierce stream of hot water to drown the sound of her soft weeping. She cried once again for the loss of Maggie Doyle and the generosity of the gallant, lonely woman living directly across Manhattan whom she would miss terribly during the next two years. And she mourned, too, the sudden, sorry state of her personal life.

Kerry slept fitfully beside Charlie, who had finally come to bed in the wee hours. She was already awake before the alarm on her cellphone was due to ring. She turned it off and bolted for the bathroom, thinking of a myriad of last-minute To Do's before the car service to the airport arrived.

She stared into the medicine cabinet mirror at her tousled head of shoulder-length, ebony hair and the royal blue eyes that distinguished her "Black Irish" ancestry, and wondered how, at thirty-three, she'd somehow lost her sex appeal? She glanced through the half-opened door at Charlie lying, face down, his head buried beneath his pillow. She realized, with a start, that they hadn't made love in—what? A month? Two? Could it be since Charlie first mentioned the possibility of selling CookChic to LifestyleXer, a deal that now sealed their joint fate?

That was it!

They'd ceased being intimate almost three months ago, right after all the negotiations to sign over their start-up to the bigger company began, and their new boss, Beverly Silverstein, insisted they make a move to San Francisco. What had appeared a solid personal-professional relationship between Charlie and her just seemed to unravel.

Kerry searched her memory for the exact moment it all seemed to go awry. Perhaps it was when her expression disclosed her dismay about the "offer they couldn't refuse"—moving to San Francisco.

At first, she'd been as excited as he was at the prospect of making some serious money for the first time in her life. But then, the thought of leaving her family, and—most of all—Angelica, now that she was both widowed and childless, plus the reality of the increased workload of writing more daily posts, along with supervising an army of bloggers around the country, began to weigh on her, and she'd summoned the courage to voice her misgivings.

"Look, Charlie…this offer sounded pretty great, at first, but when you really look at what our new bosses want from us—their demands are huge, and besides, it's really pushing me farther and farther away from what I love: which is *making* food, not writing about it!"

Charlie had been angry when she'd pointed out these negatives and responded, thin-lipped, "Look…you don't *have* to do this, you know. We can tell Beverly you just want to do your little blog from New York, and I'll recruit and manage the other blog teams from out there. We'd have to adjust the fifty-fifty deal between you and me, but—"

"*You*?" Kerry challenged, hurt he'd dismiss their relationship so casually. "You've never written or edited a piece of copy in your life."

"Exactly!" he'd replied. "See how you're about to *screw up* everything? If you really want to grab that brass ring, Kerry girl, you'd better suck it up and head west to the new Gold Rush going on out there in Silicon Land." When she'd remained silent, he'd grown impatient. "It's only for two years, for God's sake! Once the stock goes public and we vest, you're free to live wherever you damn please!"

"Can't we just say no to moving out there? Do it all from New York…and yes, I could *use* your help recruiting new bloggers!"

She could tell that Charlie had become even more exasperated with her, but he'd simmered down and merely gave a slight shrug of his black, T-shirt clad shoulders.

"Well, if you don't show them your good faith with the acquisition of CookChic before the company goes public, your *not* moving to company headquarters could actually be a deal-breaker…and wreck things for both of us."

Recalling the conversation, now, only made her feel worse, so she turned on the water in the bathroom sink and began to scrub her face.

She'd ultimately come to realize that for Charlie, it was all about the score…the "Big Bucks," as he always termed it. And it didn't really seem to matter to him how he or she got to the promised payday. Or, in her case, whether it felt right or made her happy. Just that he put a notch on his dot-com belt and that she was dumb not to do the same.

To be fair, she conceded silently, leaning over the bathroom sink to brush her teeth, Charlie Miller had taught her everything she knew about social media and building a business from scratch. She should at least give the guy some credit for that.

"Hey, you might eventually have enough money to invest in your own restaurant, kiddo!" he'd said, once the discussion was over and she'd agreed on the move. "Or you can buy out your mom and dad so they can retire"—though Charlie knew perfectly well that being partners with her brothers, Liam and Connor, at a beer and grill joint was not exactly what she had in mind.

Heaving a sigh for all the other things she *hadn't* said to Charlie to make a more convincing argument about her emotional obligations to Angelica and the other good reasons for remaining in New York, Kerry resignedly applied her lipstick and a touch of mascara to her already dark lashes. She donned the clothes she'd laid out to wear on the plane and headed through the bedroom with her remaining toiletries to pack them in her suitcase waiting in the living room.

"Charlie…wake up," she called over her shoulder. "The car will be here in twenty minutes."

By this time, Charlie had flopped over on his back, the overnight stubble on his slack jaw making it appear as if he hadn't washed his face in a very long time. His thinning brown hair had been flattened against his skull by the pillow he'd slept under, revealing a receding hairline that would be a serious detriment, one day, to his rather ascetic good looks.

"C'mon!" she repeated. "Up-and-at-'em. California here we come, right?" She was startled by her sarcastic tone. She was starting to sound just like Charlie.

Not good, she thought glumly.

She tucked her cosmetic bag into her suitcase and then spotted the airplane boarding passes Charlie had printed out after she'd gone to bed. She opened her purse to stow them where they'd be easily accessible and noticed the vintage leather ring box her godmother had given her, wedged next to her wallet.

She could hear Charlie pad toward the bathroom and soon the water was running in the shower, full blast. Meanwhile, she slowly lifted the box's lid and withdrew the Claddagh ring, her breath catching as she read the inscription engraved inside the gold band.

Know Thy Heart.

Tucked tightly against the red silk lining inside the box lid was a small, yellowed piece of paper that she unfolded, revealing a message penned in spidery script.

Be brave!—for the ring of truth will test you. Once on your finger, its power to speak endures but seven days. Listen and learn, lest you lose its wisdom and your heart's desire. When seven days pass, prepare to give the Claddagh as a gift. Once her face you see, you'll know the one who must the ring receive. On her bestow the ring of truth…

Kerry stared at the ring as she slipped it from its silk nest and onto her finger. Despite the jewelry's age and what the metal must have been subjected to on 9/11, its surface remained smooth and unblemished and the gemstone in the perfect shape of a heart. She'd put it on her right hand with the point of the heart facing outward—the age-old Irish symbol for an unmarried person who was "open to love." Within seconds, an odd tingling began to radiate up her arm as she vaguely heard Charlie humming off-key in the bathroom.

Is Charlie Miller open to love?

Startled by the suddenness of this thought, she stared

at the heart-shaped emerald, but the gemstone remained its lovely green hue. Apparently, she thought with a cynical grimace, the ring hadn't warmed up yet.

Tucking the empty ring box back into her purse, she noticed Charlie's laptop sitting on his suitcase, its battery charger plugged into both the computer and the wall. When she reached to unplug it for him, inadvertently touching the keyboard, the screen sprang to life. A glowing page from his Inbox displayed a long series of emails with the same name repeated nearly all the way down the page. Why were there so many communications these last days in New York from b.silverstein at lifestylerXer dot com that Kerry had never been copied on?

Beverly Silverstein was the executive that had let them know that closing their deal was on shaky grounds unless they agreed to move out to California until the public stock offering was final and their shares in the company fully vested.

Kerry was curious why it would have taken so many emails to Charlie to convey the facts they'd already agreed to? Or were there other elements of the new relationship between their buyer and CookChic she should have been told about? She would have been embarrassed to admit to Angelica that she'd left working out the details of their deal to Charlie and their lawyer—*his* lawyer, actually—and now she regretted not knowing much about the contract she'd signed.

Click on that name…the last entry at the top of the page…

Kerry heard her own sharp intake of breath and glanced down at her right hand. The emerald had taken on a glowing, pulsing opalescence, and waves of warmth had begun to spread up her right arm.

She shifted her gaze to Charlie's laptop and obediently clicked on the most recent email. A message instantly displayed across the screen, its date and time confirming that it was sent late the previous night.

Charlie Boy…

One last thought before u go to sleep…I cannot believe u will actually arrive in San Francisco tomorrow afternoon! Have u told KH yet? I'd just as soon have that dealt with b4 u walk into the Howard Street offices, please.

I'll have someone from r HR staff sit her down as soon as she is assigned her cubicle and explain how things r to b…

Meanwhile, lol & xoxo
Beverly

Kerry tore her gaze from the laptop as she heard Charlie's footsteps heading out of the bathroom. A jumble of emotions swinging wildly between suspicion, shock, and embarrassment for being caught reading somebody else's email propelled her across the living room to busy herself zipping up her carry-on bag.

Charlie called out, "You left a lipstick on the sink. If you want it, better come get it."

"Yeah. Right. In a minute."

Tell him what you've seen!

She didn't have to look at the Claddagh ring to know where *that* thought came from, but a quick peek confirmed it. The emerald stone now glowed a pearly white.

Then another notion floated through her head. Perhaps she was totally reading too much into that email—and only imagined that the ring had changed color since the stone had resumed its deep green hue once again. And she would have given anything to have had the time to click on some of b.silverstein's previous missives before launching any accusations at her lover and business partner. Didn't half the universe sign off "lol" and include the shorthand for "hugs and kisses?"

Charlie appeared at the doorway to the living room just as the laptop's screen reverted to sleep mode.

"C'mon!" he demanded, irritation lacing his words. "Let's move it! I just got a text that the car service is waiting downstairs. We can't be late *this* time, Kerry!"

Kerry raced into the bathroom to collect her last personal possession, chucked it into her purse, and rode in silence to the ground floor.

Don't shoot yourself in the foot, Kerry. You've got a lot riding on whatever you decide to do…keep your mouth shut until you're sure you know what's going on…

Then a louder, more insistent voice in her head declared:

Don't be daft! You know *what's going on!*

Kerry spent the entire early morning, five hour and fifty minute flight to California pretending to be asleep while her mind was whirling with a variety of scenarios about what all those emails from Beverly Silverstein meant—and none of her conclusions were good.

The central question spinning around in her head was their boss's query: "Have you told KH yet?" And why was the *tone* of the email so chummy? No…*intimate*, which was odd, given that Charlie had rarely mentioned the woman's name, once their deal papers had been signed. And what, exactly, was LifestyleXer's Human Resources Department going to inform Kerry about "how things are going to be?"

Even when she roused herself to pick at the pre-packaged airline fare of crackers and cheese, her frosty silence had the effect of keeping her seat companion mum until a sleek Lincoln Town Car, sent by their new employers, pulled up to the curb just as they came out of the Virgin America baggage area at San Francisco Airport.

Kerry watched silently as the limo driver loaded their luggage into the trunk. With the three-hour time change, it

saying? Frankly, all that stuff got kinda old."

She ignored the barbs that she knew, somehow, he was employing to insult and denigrate her, thereby giving him the upper hand. Oddly, knowing it was over with Charlie Miller produced a strange sense of relief. Even so, what a lying son-of-a-bitch!

In a low, angry voice, devoid, now, of the slightest hint of tears, she said, "And *your* usual type is your duplicitous little lab partner who's become an ace exec in the digital frenzy out here—and a convenient stepping stone to Silicon Valley for your next big score? *Nice.*"

"Hey, look, Kerry—" he began, but she hardly heard him.

"And what if I tell Ms. Silverstein's *boss* what you two have cooked up here? That she just made you part of the package so she could get her old Bronx boyfriend back?"

Charlie paused and she could tell he was choosing his words carefully.

"Listen, Kerry," he said in a conciliatory tone, "sure…I should have told you that the thing I once had with Beverly had heated up again, but when she read your blog and thought that CookChic was a perfect acquisition for her company *and* a way for her and me to be together—giving all three of us a pretty big boost, by the way—I figured it was cool since you and I would both make a nice chunk of change, and—"

"That is just *crap,* Charlie Miller!" she exploded. "You figured you'd get me out here so *you* wouldn't miss out grabbing that proverbial brass ring you kept talking about. I should have known you were a taker from the shitty way you treated Joe and Sally at our old office. Why should *I* be any different, except as your ticket west?"

"Hey, wait a minute," he countered. "You didn't know the first thing about promoting yourself as either a chef or a food expert, and you knew less than zero about driving the kind of traffic you're now getting on that blog, thanks to me! I've given you the chance to make a half million bucks or more so you can write any ticket you want in your precious food world, so don't make *me* the villain here!"

"You're not worthy of being a villain," she retorted. "You barely rise to the level of *creep*."

Kerry could see that Charlie was genuinely shocked to hear his usually polite and well-behaved former girlfriend lash back so effectively. But by this time, her initial outrage had morphed into deadly calm.

"You're right, though," she continued. "You did do all those things to promote my blog. It's just that how you've gone about it is pretty slimy, Charlie Boy."

Gazing across the limo's wide seat, she wondered how in the world she had slipped into an intimate relationship with a man who should have remained a business partner—if that, even—given the dishonest troll that her CIA classmate had turned out to be. Out of her lack of confidence in her talents as a newly-minted chef, along with sheer fear about living on her own, she'd ignored all the signs that Angelica had obviously picked up on.

Kerry glanced down at the ring on her right hand. *Know Thy heart* the Claddagh's inscription advised

She wondered, now, if she knew the first thing about hers. And if she were brutally honest, she'd learned today that she had never been in love with Charlie Miller, any more than he had been with her. She had *wanted* to be in love, but that definitely wasn't the same thing.

Then, much to her amazement, the Claddagh ring's deep green stone began to radiate an inner light until it appeared white hot.

*Keep the faith, Kerry…*wanting *to be in love is the same thing as being* open *to love…but next time, listen to your heart, instead of your head.*

***

The moment the limousine arrived at the Howard Street lobby of LifestyleXer.com, Kerry watched, dumbfounded, as Beverly Silverstein immediately took Charlie's arm, led him into an elevator, and disappeared without more than a curt nod in her direction. Meanwhile, a trim young woman in tight-fitting, straight-legged, two-hundred-dollar jeans and a boat-necked coral cashmere sweater that barely reached her midriff sashayed over to Kerry and swiftly ushered her down a deserted hallway and into a vast bullpen of wall-to-wall cubicles.

"Here is where we've set it up for you to work," announced Kerry's 'minder' who'd introduced herself as Tiffany Gergus, Assistant Director of Human Resources. "People in here are at their desks by eight o'clock, by the way," she added with a thin smile, as if she greatly enjoyed informing new hires about strict company rules.

Kerry's assigned cubicle was positioned in the middle of perhaps fifty others, all jammed cheek by jowl into the enormous room with track lighting overhead and a row of windows facing the back of the building.

"I plan to work at home a few days a week," Kerry said in a firm tone of voice. No twenty-six–year-old was going to treat her like a minor little worker bee, given the deal she'd signed with this company.

Ms. Gergus arched an eyebrow.

"We've tightened up the WAH rules, so I'm afraid we expect you to be in that chair *every* morning by eight."

"WAH rules?" Kerry repeated, furrowing her brow. "Oh…you mean 'working at home.' WAH."

Ms. Gergus cast her a look of disdain as if everyone in the Universe knew that WAH stood for working-at-home. Then she pronounced with steely officiousness, "And also, Kerry, I see there was an addendum to your contract last week that stipulates you're to blog 500 to 800 words on food, travel, and restaurant subjects twice a day, and once on Saturday."

"*What?*" Kerry exclaimed, and sensed her cube-mates were all ears. "I never agreed to posting on Saturday!"

The young woman smiled primly.

"You certainly did. I just read your personal services contract word-for-word this morning, before you arrived. Mr. Miller, as president of your former company, signed that addition and said you'd okayed it."

"Well, I didn't," Kerry retorted.

The HR assistant narrowed her gaze.

"Well, then I suggest you'd better speak to Beverly about it."

Beverly, is it? It was definitely more than "casual Friday" if a lowly assistant spoke of a company vice president in such a familiar way.

"Also, the vice president wants a full report by a week, tomorrow, on how many new bloggers you've recruited in the major markets, as outlined in your deal."

She had a week *to find food bloggers in ten cities as experienced as she was?*

Impossible.

Tiffany Gergus pursed her lips and said by means of farewell, "And a final few things you should know…I want to be sure it's clear to you that your stock options do not vest for a full two years after this company tenders its announced Initial Public Offering three weeks from now and, after that, you can only sell your shares in twenty-five percent increments—"

"Yes, Tiffany," Kerry interrupted, deliberately calling the little twit by her first name. "I'm sure Ms. Silverstein told you to emphasize that fact, but I'm well aware of standard, boilerplate regulations about selling company stock."

As if Kerry hadn't uttered a word, the HR representative continued, "And, I hope you are aware that your contract also stipulates that if Ms. Silverstein doesn't find your blogging up to par, you could be out-placed before that date."

Kerry stared at the assured young woman, unable to mask her astonishment. She *hadn't* realized that little feature must have been in the fine print somewhere.

Tiffany slapped down on the empty desk something that looked like a credit card with Kerry's photo on it that LifeStyleXer must have scraped off the CookChic website.

"Here's your ID that will also serve as your cafeteria card. You get the first hundred dollars of food free every month."

Before Kerry could reply, the young woman handed her a thick manila envelope. "And just so you won't bother a busy executive like Beverly about any of the other details in your revised employment agreement, I made you a copy and I suggest you read it very carefully…line by line."

Without so much as a farewell, Ms. Tiffany Gergus turned on her Kate Spade wedge-heeled sandals and marched toward the exit. Kerry noted that the Human Resources assistant was not offered a single friendly wave from anyone encased in the other cubicles that the tight-assed woman walked past on her way out.

Chapter Three

Alone in her cubicle, Kerry stared at the contract she'd trustingly signed on Charlie's assurances that it was "practically a free giveaway," reeling from the shock of having read it thoroughly and understanding, now, that the terms were far more advantageous to the parent company than to CookChic. Unable to think clearly about what she should do next, she made her way to the company cafeteria with the desperate hope that wine was sold with lunch.

The ultra-modern steel-and-glass expanse featured food stations with every imaginable cuisine provided to fuel workers who toiled the long hours that employment at LifeStyleXer apparently required. Sometimes, according to a cynical cube-mate named Jason who'd provided directions to the cafeteria, he slept under his desk when a new feature of the website was due to be launched. "It's way cool that it's open twenty-four/seven."

Kerry noted the variety of ethnic choices: Thai, Chinese, Japanese, to say nothing of fragrant Indian curry and the heavenly aroma of Tandoori chicken, along with the sweet scent of steaming jasmine rice. Kerry had begun to feel queasy from her sleepless night and the flight across the country—to say nothing of the full scope of the upsetting situation that faced her, now that she'd read every word of her contract. She stood in line at the made-to-order salad bar in hopes that eating something light would settle her stomach.

"Next?" called out a short, dark-haired young man wearing a nameplate that identified him as "Tony Perez,

Salad Associate."

"I'll take the Arugula Carpaccio, please, with the raspberry balsamic dressing on the side."

The cafeteria worker gazed curiously across the counter. "Best choice we offer," he complimented her, adding, "You just got here, right? You're the new food blogger we just bought?"

Kerry gave a short laugh. "Well, yes…I do sort of feel as if I've been bought and sold. How'd you guess?"

He pointed at the ID around her neck.

"*And* you ordered the arugula with thin-sliced beef. Half the people who work here claim they're vegetarians or vegans, and besides, it's a new item and nobody wants to take a chance until I can tell them it's a favorite with some of the bigwigs." Tony Perez grinned as he began to assemble her order. "Also, I saw the announcement on the company website last week. Only a foodie would know what a killer salad this is," he said, his smile growing even wider. "I only added it to the menu on Monday."

Kerry smiled back, cheered by Tony's enthusiasm for his work as she took the plate piled high with fresh greens, topped with paper-thin slices of grass-fed beef—or so the menu card on the glass case asserted

"I'll let you know how I like it, but it looks wonderful."

"And tell me what you think of the salad dressing. It's made with locally-produced olive oil and raspberries from an organic farm just north of here."

Kerry was immediately intrigued.

"You sound very knowledgeable about what's going on in this neck of the woods. Can you give me the contact info for the local olive oil producer you mentioned?"

Tony shrugged. "Sure…I'll come over to your table before you leave. I'm just getting off my shift." He glanced at the clock that registered two p.m. "In fact, I was thinking about going over to Berkeley later this afternoon to pick up a case of Montisi Olive Oil at Amphora Nueva. Rumors are, they're just delivering their latest press."

"Really? It's just been released?"

"Yeah. The Montisi ranch is up north, near Petaluma, forty minutes from here in Sonoma." Tony hesitated and then blurted, "Wanna come with me to Berkeley? The olive oil store is fantastic! You won't believe how much stuff they stock from all over the world!"

The brash young man was obviously eager to make friends with his company's latest acquisition, despite his lowly status as "salad associate." Kerry admired his moxie. And besides, it appeared as if he might be well connected to the food scene in the Bay Area. She was already worried about keeping up with the crazy deadlines stipulated by the sweatshop contract she'd unwittingly signed.

She smiled at Tony. "The olive oil store sounds like it might make for a good first blog post, but you'd better let me see how I like the salad. Talk to you in a bit."

Kerry headed for a small table-for-two positioned away from the other diners. She was not in the mood to meet or talk to any of her fellow slaves. However, her spirits perked up the instant she sampled Tony Perez's leafy concoction. The fresh, peppery arugula was complemented by the full-flavored slices of delicious *carpaccio*, and the entire assemblage was wrapped in a smooth slurry of rich, fragrant olive oil with an after-burner hit of raspberry-flavored balsamic vinegar.

It was *brilliant*!

She was just rising from her chair to find Tony when the young man came bounding over.

"Well?" he demanded.

"It's absolutely wonderful!" she declared. "The blending of flavors and textures is first rate, and the *freshness* of all the ingredients—"

"Then you wanna go over to Berkeley with me? The people at Amphora Nueva are kinda friends of mine. They sell only the best stuff—and can tell you all about the scams in the olive oil biz!"

Tony's enthusiasm was infectious, but first she had to have it out with Charlie about the Addendum that he'd signed in her stead without telling her.

"What's your cell number?" she asked. "I just checked into my cube and I have a few things I need to take care of. Can I call you and let you know if I can make it? If not today, then I'd love to go there with you another time."

Tony whipped out his cell, got her email address and phone number, and sent her his contact information as well.

"I need to leave by no later than three-fifteen," he warned, "otherwise the traffic across the Bay Bridge is killer."

Kerry nodded, her thoughts careening between several story ideas based on what Tony had told her and her burning desire to tell Charlie Miller exactly what she thought of him for the second time in a single day.

"I'll call you either way," she promised. "And thanks! You've been the nicest thing that's happened since I got here."

Kerry figured that the quickest route to finding Charlie in the huge office complex was to ask for directions to Vice President Beverly Silverstein's office. Once there, however, another junior assistant type leapt up from a chair inside the glass-fronted conference room where Kerry spotted Charlie, along with their mutual boss and several other jeans-clad whiz kids, as well as a man who *might* have been approaching fifty.

Kerry wondered if the adult supervisor-looking guy was LifeStyleXer's CEO, Harry Chapman, gathered with his inner circle around the polished, oval glass table where one of their number was giving a Power Point presentation with a display of brightly colored pie charts.

Kerry heard a whoosh of air as a painfully thin young guard dog pushed open the conference room's glass door and rushed toward her before Kerry could rap her knuckles on the transparent wall and embarrass Charlie so he'd come out in the hall.

"I'm sorry, but you can't go in there…they're in a meeting," the twig of a woman added, stating the obvious. She swiftly handed Kerry an envelope as if she somehow knew the visitor was due to arrive. "Beverly said to give you this."

Startled, Kerry stared at the missive the young woman had practically shoved into her hands.

"What *is* this?"

"Your housing voucher for the W Hotel down the street. You have two weeks free lodging until you find a place to live," she said with a bright smile.

"*Two weeks*?" Kerry protested. "In a city with a zero vacancy rate and eleven blog deadlines from hell? That's ridiculous! Where will Charlie Miller and I keep our furniture when it arrives from New York?" she demanded.

Glancing worriedly over her shoulder, Beverly Silverstein's messenger grabbed Kerry by the arm and with surprising force for an anorexic, guided her a few feet down the hall toward the elevator.

"Shhh…there are some high-level discussions going on in there about the IPO!" she admonished. "I was told that Charlie would help you sort out your belongings when they came and—"

"*Charlie!*" she echoed, shocked that an underling would be on a first-name basis with an employee who had arrived less than two hours earlier. "How the hell do *you* know what that rat man Charlie Miller would or wouldn't do?"

She glared over her shoulder at the man himself who, by this time, had turned in his chair and was staring nervously back at her.

Kerry held his glance for a long moment as a warm, pulsing sensation flooded up her arm. She glanced down at the Claddagh ring whose center had turned pearly white.

Smile sweetly and make a dignified retreat!

The voice in her head was adamant and she chose, at that moment, to believe it was her own good sense that advised her to get away from the conference room as fast as her legs would carry her before she decked the young woman now clutching her other arm.

"Ah…okay, then," she said, tugging free.

For some reason she had a moment's sympathy for the messenger who had been tasked to give her such an ignominious brush-off. At a mere twenty-something, the poor, skinny excuse for a human being had already sold her soul.

Kerry somehow summoned a smile.

"You try to have a nice day, won't you?" she addressed her latest minder. "And when you get something to eat after the meeting—and I hope that you *will*—try the arugula and *carpaccio* salad in the cafeteria. It's fabulous!"

Kerry made fast work of checking into her assigned room at the W Hotel on Third and Howard streets where a reservation had been made in her name—only—by "LifeStyleXer's Vice President, Beverly Silverstein, *herself,*" the desk clerk admiringly informed the new guest. "I hear that's a cool company to work for," she added, noting, "I'm just finishing up my degree in computer science at SF State. Could I get in touch with you, Ms.—" she glanced down at the registration, "…Ms. Hannigan, when I graduate? Maybe you could put in a good word?"

Still steaming that Charlie's latest girlfriend had plotted every aspect of their arrival in San Francisco, Kerry grabbed her key card off the front desk and snapped,

"Contact Beverly Silverstein directly and see how much she helps *you*!"

By three o'clock, she had unpacked her belongings, reached Tony Perez by mobile phone, and was standing curbside when a battered VW Jetta drew up to the hotel's entrance.

"Hop in…we gotta get over the bridge before it's bumper to bumper," he directed.

Traffic was sluggish, but moving, as they crossed the four-and-a-half mile expanse of water separating San Francisco from the East Bay communities of Oakland—and a few miles further north—Berkeley, the university community nestled into hillsides with spectacular views back to the city. Then a thought struck her.

"Isn't the Bay Bridge the one that collapsed in the earthquake?" she asked, suddenly apprehensive as she gazed out the car window at the enormous body of water whizzing by below.

"Way back in 1989," he assured her cheerfully, "but they've done a retrofit."

"Oh. Great. So…Tony," she asked, wanting not to think about either the bridge, incipient earthquakes, or the impossible situation that had so suddenly been thrust upon her today, "tell me, how did you became Salad Man at LifestyleXer?"

Tony, his eyes on the road, gave a short laugh.

"My parents were field workers, you know? From Mexico. I was the eldest, so I grew up making the meals for everyone in my family when they crawled home at the end of the day, down in Castroville." Tony paused, adding with a big grin, "You know Castroville, dontcha? 'Artichoke Capitol of the World?'"

Kerry nodded. She'd done her research about the agricultural bounty in California.

"Well, even as a little kid, I always liked to cook," he said with a shrug, "and when I flunked out of community college because I hated it—and I couldn't afford culinary school—I decided two years ago to get hands-on experience, here in the city, and learn as much as I can while I keep an ear out for a job at one of the top restaurants." He looked across the passenger seat and grimaced. "I know that sounds pretty cocky…that I could go from a cafeteria to a name restaurant…but I think I'm really good."

Kerry thought with a stab of guilt how Angelica had cheerfully spent more than fifty thousand dollars on Kerry's tuition at the CIA, and here was a guy willing to slave in a cafeteria to be able to do what he loved.

"Well…based on that salad of yours I ate today, I don't think you're too cocky at all. I'm guessing that you have everything it takes to become a great chef."

Tony's tanned complexion took on a glow, his pleasure at hearing her words obvious.

"Wow! And coming from *you*…double wow! Thanks! And *I* guess this is the time I should admit I am a huge fan of your CookChic blog…and have been ever since you began posting."

Kerry was pleased by the fact that her blogs might be educating the next generation of great chefs and his kind words assuaged her guilt, somewhat, about not directly putting to use what she'd learned at the CIA.

Tony wound his car up Ashby Avenue, climbing successively higher into the Berkeley Hills with each turn in the road. At length, he made a left on Domingo and parked in the shadow of the massive Claremont Hotel, a shingled extravaganza from another era, he explained, that still hosted weddings and temporarily housed well-heeled out-of-towners visiting the UC Berkeley campus.

They parked and entered the cool confines of the "Amphora Nueva Olive Oil Works," as it said on the business card Kerry grabbed from the counter. In the next moment, she heard a man's voice call out at the rear of the shop to someone entering from the service door.

"Hey, Ren! Great to see ya! That's your latest? Well then, just wheel that dolly right in here, my friend. I can't wait to taste that first press of yours! We've all been waiting with bated breath."

"We are *so* in luck!" Tony whispered loudly. "The rumors were true! That's Renato Montisi *himself* back there," he added excitedly, nodding in the direction of the rear of the large room that had rows of two-foot-high stainless steel olive oil dispensers lined along the wall. "Montisi Ranch usually presses their olives in mid-to-late November, and then delivers soon after, and I guessed right. Today's the *day*!"

The store's proprietor walked up to the tall, good-looking figure he had hailed as "Ren" who had wheeled in his dolly loaded with a large, stainless steel drum. Printed on its circumference was an olive branch logo and the words MONTISI RANCH OLIVE OIL.

From across the store, Kerry absorbed the view of the six-foot, broad-shouldered man delivering his wares and felt an unexpected flutter in her chest at the sight of his full head of dark blond, wind-blown hair that was barely tamed by a pair of pricey Ray Ban sunglasses perched just above his tanned forehead. About her age—or perhaps a few years older—his high cheekbones and square jaw, along with trim arms that were also tanned despite its being early December, made him appear more like a sought-after ski instructor than a rancher. She could also easily imagine him in an expensive suit and tie, addressing an audience in the LifestyleXer boardroom. Yet, here he was, wearing jeans, work boots, and a brown T-shirt with the same Montisi Ranch logo stamped in khaki green across a muscular chest that couldn't help but capture a bystander's attention.

"Hey, how's everybody doing?" Ren asked of store owner Michael Bradley and his staff that had gathered in a circle around the dolly. "Yep, this is our latest press. Do you have some bread to give it a taste?"

"C'mon!" exhorted Tony in a harsh whisper. "Let's get in line!" He grabbed her arm and hustled toward the small crowd in the back. "Hi," he boldly addressed the group. "I'm Tony Perez and this is Kerry Hannigan, who just moved to San Francisco from New York. She's the CookChic food blogger and I brought her here because maybe she'll do a post about your latest product, Mr. Montisi…and also about the store," he added hastily to the owner of Amphora Nueva.

Both men turned to stare at the interlopers while Kerry could feel her pale complexion flush with color. She was embarrassed by Tony's brashness and a promise she'd write a blog about a new product she hadn't even tasted yet.

"Oh, please," she protested. "We don't mean to interrupt…"

The man who had just delivered his latest harvest met her glance and a moment later was smiling broadly.

"You're not interrupting," he said, extending his hand in greeting. As soon as Kerry felt his palm wrapped around hers, she sensed a curious vibration traveling from the ring finger of her right hand, straight to her chest. "I'm Ren Montisi, and—as a matter of fact—I subscribe to your blog, so I'm very aware that you know your stuff." He cast her a confident smile, releasing her hand. "You're just in time to give me your opinion of this year's first press."

"I…love olive oil, but I'm certainly no tasting expert—"

"All I want is your unvarnished reaction as a consumer. We bottled this only last week."

Their eyes met and Kerry realized she was actually holding her breath. A strange current of… *what*? Excitement? Anticipation? Whatever the sensation was, Kerry had felt a second tremor pass from Ren's hand to her solar plexus.

"S-sure…" she managed to stammer. "I'll tell you what I think…honestly," she added in the name of journalism.

He took a few small cubes from a basket of bread cut from a French baguette that the store owner had handed him and offered one to her and another to Tony. Then he put a small porcelain saucer beneath the spigot on the steel drum and allowed a stream of green-golden olive oil to fill halfway to the rim.

"Everybody ready?" he asked, his gaze making a sweep of his audience. Despite his smile, Kerry thought she noticed tension gathering at the corners of his generous mouth.

By this time, several other customers had joined the small throng, each holding a cube of bread between forefinger and thumb. Kerry leaned forward, followed eagerly by Tony Perez, and dipped her sourdough into the pool of oil, watching the bread quickly absorb the liquid like a miniature sponge.

She turned away from the group, popped the small square into her mouth, and allowed the bread and dripping oil to slide over her tongue. At first, there was a fresh, familiar taste of olives, soon followed by a sparkling, peppery finish she found utterly delicious. Like Tony's raspberry salad dressing, it was one of the most wonderful flavors she'd ever tasted!

She turned back and again locked glances with the creator of this liquid gold. Eyes wide with astonishment at the complex flavors flooding her taste buds, she continued to slowly chew the bread and finally swallowed it.

"Oh…wow," she pronounced on a long breath. "Oh, *really* wow! I have never tasted anything like this in my life!" She laughed and pointed to the big stainless steel drum, addressing the owner of Amphora Nueva. "Can you please decant about ten bottles of that for me?" she asked. "No, make that an even dozen."

Ren Montisi was blatantly staring, eyes crinkling with relief he couldn't disguise.

"No!" she assured him quickly, "I really mean it. I want to send this amazing stuff to friends as this year's Christmas presents, instead of wine." She took a step forward and gazed into amber eyes of variegated shades that reminded her of the colors in Central Park each autumn. With those amazing eyes and Ren's dark blond hair, she speculated that the original Montisis must hail from mid-to-north Italy. She held his glance and said, "I truly think this may be the best olive oil on the planet."

"Have you been to Tuscany?" Ren asked.

"Yes, but I never tasted anything like this."

"Sometime, go to the little village of Montisi—not far from Montepulciano—about forty miles south of Siena," he said, flashing a dazzling grin as he confirmed her conjecture about his family's origins. "The oil from the original Montisi groves rivals this…almost," he added, continuing to look at her with unnerving interest, which prompted her to glance down at the Claddagh ring, rather than drown in his steady gaze. Its stone was pure white and pulsing.

Ask for an interview. Go see the ranch where the oil is produced!

Kerry was about to open her mouth to repeat these thoughts aloud when Ren said, "Why don't you come see where we make this? We're hosting a bunch of food writers like yourself at the ranch tomorrow, which means you'll probably feel right at home. I'm sure Chef Jeremy can make room for one more place setting."

She glanced over her shoulder at Tony. "Tony Perez and I work for the same company now. He's in charge of salads at the LifestyleXer dot com cafeteria and is a big fan of your oil."

Ren's smile faded and he said, "Oh…well…perhaps since it's two of you—"

Tony shook his head sorrowfully. "I gotta work tomorrow, but Kerry can tell me all about it. It's her very first day in California, Mr. Montisi, and she can't miss out on something like this."

Kerry observed another of Ren Montisi's faintly devastating grins spread across his handsome features as he turned to the owner of Amphora Nueva.

"Well, now, why don't we decant thirteen bottles of Montisi's finest for these nice folks?"

Ten minutes later, Ren fished into his back jean's pocket and brought out a business card imprinted with his ranch's logo that he handed to the young woman with the shoulder-length, jet black hair and totally arresting sapphire eyes. He couldn't believe his luck running into one of the major food bloggers in the country. And what a stunner! What was she doing in *this* store on *this* day, he marveled?

"Here's where you come tomorrow," he explained. "Do you think you can find your way to us? On a Saturday, it should take you about forty-fifty minutes up Highway 101 from the city. We'll be serving wine and iced tea and a few things to nibble on at twelve and we'll sit down to lunch at about quarter to one."

He'd never wanted anyone to accept an invitation to see the ranch as much in his life as he did Kerry Hannigan. Jeremy had been the first to talk about her blog and her philosophy about how America should eat food grown close to its source. "The Hundred-Mile Diet" had become a cliché in Northern California, at least, but the woman standing only a few feet from him had a way of telling stories within her blog posts that won his rapt attention and admiration from the first time he'd read her work.

He would never admit to anyone that he'd studied her picture on her website late one evening, but it was nothing compared to seeing first hand that lovely pale skin with cheeks that blushed when she was excited, as he'd observed earlier when she'd tasted the oil-infused cube of bread. And despite all the food she must consume for her job, she had a slender figure, but one with curves right where they should be. She couldn't be more than five-feet-four, which was so different from—

He didn't want to make comparisons. Studying Kerry Hannigan's every gesture, he had the strangest inclination to take her in his arms to see if she'd fit snugly under his chin…

She was talking to him now, he realized with a start.

"Would it be possible to show up at your ranch…say, at ten-thirty," she inquired politely, "so I could do a quick interview and you could show me the olive groves and your production facility before the hordes arrive? And may I take some photos for my blog?"

"Absolutely, but can you make that eight-thirty?" Ren countered and then grimaced. "I know that's ridiculously early, but I've got to be on tap for my staff getting ready for that big busload of your fellow writers due to arrive sometime before noon. That way, we can walk the groves and see the vegetable garden and the lavender fields, and then sit down in my office with some coffee to talk before things get too hectic."

"Perfect!" she exclaimed, and he was exhilarated to see by the color staining her cheeks, evidence that she was clearly excited at the prospect of visiting the ranch.

"And if you have a tight deadline tomorrow," he ventured, "while we wait for the other food writers to arrive—or after they depart—you can use my computer, if you want or need to. I'll be busy being the genial host."

He was determined to offer the woman every courtesy to smooth the way for a possible mention in her influential blog. If she used his office, he thought with a sudden sense of pleasure that raised his flagging spirits, she'd hang around the ranch a little longer and that would be great on its own merits.

Ren struggled to bring his thoughts back to the business at hand. A relieved expression lit up her lovely features.

"Borrowing your computer would be a huge help," she said. "I've just been assigned an extra blog post every Saturday, so I'll definitely take you up on your offer after everyone leaves, if I may."

"It'll be all yours," he said with a laugh. "By then I'll be on cleanup duty."

It seemed like some sort of miracle that this amazingly talented star of the food world wanted to tour his family's domestic olive oil operation and taste Jeremy's wonderful food made from ingredients grown within steps of their commercial kitchen.

Finally, he thought, the Montisi Olive Ranch and its manager might be getting a few breaks, as a spreadsheet flashed through his mind with some discouraging profit-and-loss totals at the bottom.

For Kerry's part, Renato Montisi would have been amazed to know what was whirling in her head as the clerk assembled the bottles of olive oil on the desk and began to wrap each one for transport to her friends and relatives on the East Coast.

Her mind was filled with a sense of what she could only describe as unbridled euphoria. Thanks to this astounding meet-up, not only would she get to interview the personable producer of a wonderful artisanal product, she'd also meet a raft of fellow food writers in *person,* instead of merely online. Even better, she already knew she'd get at least three or four blog posts out of seeing the olive groves, the bottling facility, and dining with nationally known culinary critics. Maybe she could even *recruit* some of them to do what she did, but in their own cities?

Relief swept over her at the thought that in one fell swoop, she could make her first week's crushing deadlines and suggest some viable names with whom to launch the LifestyleXer/CookChic brand in ten major markets, as she was contractually obligated.

And it had all happened on her first day in California! She glanced at her right hand. Surely the Claddagh ring couldn't take credit for *everything*?

Tony broke into her jumble of thoughts.

"You can borrow my car tomorrow," he offered, almost worshipfully, his attention glued—not on her—but on the bottles of olive oil that Amphora Nueva's proprietor had already decanted and had handed to him, corks firmly in place.

"Thanks," Kerry replied, turning to offer her new friend her heartfelt appreciation. "That's very sweet of you, but I'll just lease a rental." To Ren Montisi she added, "This is *so* nice of you to make time for me, given all that you have to do tomorrow. I'm really grateful—and I absolutely love your olive oil!"

She lowered her eyes with embarrassment in reaction to Ren's look of mild amazement. Was he so unaccustomed to such high praise for his wonderful product, she wondered?

He's intrigued with you, *you ninny!*

Startled, she glanced down again at her right hand in time to see the ring wink in a flash of white. She moved closer to the counter where she gave the clerk a credit card for the twelve bottles that had been filled for her at the back of the store, and then insisted on paying for Tony's as well.

"You told me about this place and drove us here," she announced firmly.

She seized the pen to sign the purchase slip and couldn't help but notice that the ring's emerald gemstone had once again turned opalescent. The next thing she knew, the voice in her head rang out for the third time since entering the shop.

Good going, my girl! Today's events will prove excellent for more than just your blog…

On Saturday morning, Kerry was thankful for her rental car's GPS that easily guided her through the empty streets at seven-thirty a.m. in downtown San Francisco to the Golden Gate Bridge that led north to Marin and Sonoma counties. She felt a thrill as the two orange-colored steel towers rose up, reassuring beacons that she was on the right road. She gave a quick glance to her left and took in the wide expanse of the Pacific Ocean where the morning sun spread a layer of gold stretching all the way to China, it seemed. On her right side, the enormous oval that was San Francisco Bay was dotted with a few large and small craft making ivory trails in the churning waters around Alcatraz and Angel islands.

Less than forty minutes later, just as Renato Montisi had directed, she took the exit before Petaluma Boulevard and followed successively narrower roads through gently rolling hills dotted with oak trees and cattle, until she spotted a wooden sign carved with bas-relief olives on a branch of a tree. She made a left turn down a tarmac road that wound into its own eight-hundred-acre valley with groves of sage-green olive trees marching up and down the hills on either side of her car.

Kerry inhaled deeply of air scented faintly with lavender and rosemary and thought she'd landed squarely in some uncharted corner of heaven. At the next bend in the road she noted that an entire field was planted, not with olive trees, but with rows and rows of lavender bushes, devoid of blooms in December, but stately in the way their sage stalks blew gently in the morning breeze.

She passed through a pair of stone stanchions, drove another quarter mile on hard-packed dirt, rolled to a stop on a wide, gravel turn-round and spotted Ren, once again clad in jeans and work boots. Today, he looked handsomer than ever in a collared, dark green polo shirt, no doubt worn in honor of the impending arrival of the nation's top food writers.

He advanced toward her across the parking area in front of a low-slung, corrugated steel building she assumed housed the olive pressing facility. Two Labradors—one black, one chocolate-colored—danced excitedly around their master.

"Meet Scusi and Prego," he announced as she emerged from her car's driver side. He pointed to his left. "Ciao, the barn cat, is in the lavender bushes over there. C'mon, hop into my truck for the Grand Tour. The dogs will follow us and get some exercise as I show you the ranch."

Kerry gingerly climbed into his truck's cab, happy she'd decided against wearing a sundress and sling-back heels in favor of a tapered pair of navy trousers, rubber-soled red flats, and a navy-and-white striped sweater with a red cardigan slung across her shoulders.

"It's really great you're willing to spend some time with me at such an early hour and before that gaggle of food critics descends on you for lunch."

"Best part of the day," he said, briefly glancing across the truck's passenger seat and offering her a mildly rueful grimace. "Actually, I was worried because my chef was a bit under the weather this week, but everything seems well in hand this morning." He piloted his khaki colored pickup truck along a road flanked by an expanse of olive trees in all directions. "Ah…" he said, pointing through the windshield, "here's the view I wanted you to see."

The pair exited the truck and stood on a rise that offered a panoramic vista of gentle hills intersected by even more rows of mature olive trees. The groves were bordered by another collection of waist-high lavender bushes.

"The flowers make their appearance in May and June, as do swarms of bees which, as you probably know, are essential to propagating all sorts of things we grow here."

Kerry concluded that the plants' mere presence accounted for the faint scent in the air she had detected earlier and that she loved so much. In the distance were several more lavender fields, "to encourage as many bees as possible to visit us," he elaborated.

She cast a sweeping gaze at the entire landscape and said softly, "We could be in Tuscany right now. It's…just gorgeous." She glanced sideways and was struck by the faintly Roman cast to Ren's profile. "I bet your family couldn't believe this scenery when they first saw it."

"Exactly right," he answered, indicating they should continue down the dirt road on foot. "The story goes that the minute that my great-grandfather, Renato Montisi, Senior, arrived from Italy and saw this land just before the turn of the twentieth century, he and his wife had just enough money to buy ten acres. Every cent he earned thereafter went into purchasing the other seven hundred and ninety."

"So your grandparents and parents chose to raise olives, too, instead of grapes?" asked Kerry. "Isn't it pretty rare that a family business survives more than three generations?"

"Well, in our case, it didn't," Ren replied, staring off into the distance. "Except for naming me after *his* grandfather, my father was the rebel. Went to law school at Cal and wanted nothing much to do with ranching after that." He paused and then continued. "Both my parents died in a private plane crash flying out of Palm Springs in bad weather. I came to live here with Nona Concetta when I was twelve. My grandfather, Renato, Junior, died three years ago, so I chucked Silicon Valley—which, trust me—I was only too happy to do," he added with a grim smile, "and took on the management of the ranch from my grandmother, who will be ninety-two next year."

Kerry thought of Angelica and how much she missed her already, wondering what Ren's grandmother was like, a woman a decade older?

By this time, Prego and Scusi had caught up with them and followed in their wake down a steep section of the road that ended in a small creek bed at the bottom of the ravine.

Kerry stole a quick look at her host's left hand and asked, "And so…you are the third Renato Montisi, yes? Is there a Renato Quattro you'll be training to take over here someday?"

After all, not every man wore a wedding ring.

Ren shot her a puzzled look. "You're asking am I married, and do I have children?"

Kerry flushed, embarrassed by her obvious probe. She expected some sort of scolding jolt to shoot up her arm from the Claddagh ring, but felt no such sensation. Before she could apologize, however, Ren turned to meet her glance.

"Yes, I was married, but no children. My wife died several years ago as a result of a skiing accident."

"Oh," she said on a swift intake of breath. "Oh, I am *so* sorry, Ren. You've lost your parents *and* your wife, and your grandfather, too. That's awful…and I apologize for bringing it up. I was just being a nosy reporter."

She was startled when he placed his hand on her arm and gave a slight shake of the head.

"You don't need to apologize. You wanted to know about the ranch and my role here. It's fine. Really."

Once again, at his touch, a strange tingling spread up her arm and the moment seemed suspended in space as if they'd slipped off the time wheel and were simply *there* together with clear, crystalline space surrounding them.

Ren turned and pointed. The tree-filled hills came back into focus.

"Would you like to see how honest olive oil is made?" he asked.

All Kerry could manage was to offer a slight nod and follow him back uphill to where he'd parked his pickup truck.

Chapter Four

Kerry's breathing had almost returned to normal by the time they'd driven back to the gravel parking lot. Once inside the bottling facility, Ren gave her a quick rundown about the process of the mill turning olives into Montisi Extra Virgin Olive Oil.

"These large stainless steel troughs are where the olives are separated from the leaves and branches, washed, and eventually pressed by that large, revolving stone disk over there that crushes the fruit and extracts the liquid," he explained.

"Olives are considered fruits, aren't they?"

"Yep. They grow on trees and have pits, so they qualify," he said with a laugh. "This first pressing—done 'cold' without heat or chemicals and hence, the term 'Extra Virgin'—eventually ends up in large vats before being decanted into bottles like the ones you purchased at Amphora Nueva, or the oil is stored in stainless steel drums."

"Like the one I saw you deliver to them yesterday, yes?"

Ren nodded, continuing, "Unlike wine, olive oil is best when used as soon after it's harvested as possible." He pointed to a bottle sitting on a nearby counter. "See…we stamp the *harvest* date, not the bottling date—which, with some outfits, can be a couple of *years* after the olives are picked and pressed." He pointed to a back shelf. "There are a few dusty bottles sitting there from a couple of years that are probably rancid by now."

"Is it true there is a certain amount of fraud and misleading advertising in your business?" she asked, suddenly putting on her reporter's hat.

"Just read Tom Mueller's book *Extra Virginity* and you'll learn all you need to know about that subject."

Kerry nodded. "I read the original piece Mueller did for *The New Yorker*, which got him the book contract, I heard. So you agree with his analysis?"

Ren grimaced. "Not only do I agree, I'm living with the consequences of my product being undercut by mislabeled olive oil posing as Extra Virgin…but that's a longer conversation." He stole a glance at his wristwatch. "Want to have a quick tour of the ranch's kitchen garden? Then, I've really got to check in with our chef and staff about today's lunch."

"Are you sure you have time to show it to me? You could just point me in the right direction and then direct me to your office. I promise I'll stay out of your way until my fellow foodies arrive." She was grateful that he had been willing to spend so much time with her, given the imminent arrival of some serious VIPs.

"We've just got time. I want you to see every carrot and herb plant, 'cause I'm hoping you get at least five blogs out of what you've seen today," he teased, pointing toward a screen door and guiding her outside the olive mill and into the parking lot again.

All during their tour she had been snapping photos on her iPhone and paused to take a picture of Scuzi, Prego, and the barn cat named Ciao. The three animals were outside the building waiting patiently for Ren to reappear.

"If these cute guys have any specific jobs around the ranch, I can even do a blog about *them*," she proposed, a giddy feeling of sheer happiness bubbling in her chest at the sight of Ren's faithful companions. She adored animals, but had never been allowed to have a pet as a child in Manhattan. And Charlie had been allergic to anything with four feet—or so he said.

"Scuzi and Prego are actually very effective watchdogs and chase off their fair share of coyotes and raccoons, and Ciao is in charge of catching mice wherever she finds them."

Kerry quickly snapped a series of pet portraits. "I'll post their story next Saturday," she said, chuckling, "but today's blog will definitely be about the food writers lunch."

That'll take care of that pesky extra blog they expect you to do!

Kerry didn't have time to speculate whose pronouncement had just sailed through her mind as she concentrated on keeping up with Ren's long strides leading toward the magnificent vegetable and fruit garden laid out at the back of a cluster of one-story buildings that served the various activities at the ranch.

"We planted half an acre of mostly vegetables a few steps from the door to our big kitchen where the food for the ranch's special events is prepared," he explained.

They had only walked twenty feet along the path that cut between the herb beds and pole bean plots when Kerry heard Ren's cellphone emit an insistent sound. He fished the device out of his jeans pocket and stared at a text.

"Oh boy…this is *not* good."

"What?" Kerry said.

Ren's voice conveyed his alarm. He showed her his text message.

Major emergency. Chef sick.

"Oh, no! Do you have a sous chef?" Kerry asked, knowing precisely how dire this situation could be, given that a busload of national food writers were due at the ranch within a few hours.

He punched in a text message.

"Yes, I've just told Jeremy's assistant, Sara Lang, to call for an ambulance."

"How far along is your prep?"

"Let's go see," Ren said, heading toward the kitchen door some fifty feet from where they were standing. "Jeremy Garafola is a terrific chef and a great guy and he'd never—"

By this time, they had both burst into the main room of the separate building that housed the kitchen, only to see a large bald-headed man in white chef's attire doubled over on a bench next to the farmhouse dining table. At the sink stood a stocky young Mexican-American who was washing dishes. As they entered, he cast his employer a worried glance.

Meanwhile, a woman about Kerry's age with long blond pigtails draped down the back of her white chef's jacket like a cast member from *Little House on the Prairie* was yelling into the phone attached to a nearby wall.

"Well, how *long* before you can get here?" she demanded shrilly. "We need *help* with this Goddamned luncheon, Tommy! I can't do this all by myself. Jeremy is toast! We're waiting for an ambulance, you jerk! Well, screw *you*!" And she slammed down the receiver.

"Take it easy, Sara," Ren admonished sharply, and then leaned over to bring his face even with Jeremy who was clutching his midsection and gasping with pain.

"God, I'm sorry, boss. This came on so suddenly. One minute I was fine, and the next—"

"It's going to be all right, buddy," Ren reassured him. "Just hold on. The Sonoma County cavalry is on its way, right, Sara?"

"Well, I hope so!" she snapped. "I called them right after you texted back." She turned her attention toward Kerry. "Who are *you*?" she demanded. "I want this kitchen clear of visitors, Ren! We have enough problems without—"

"This is Kerry Hannigan," Ren cut in. "She's a graduate of the CIA and a well-known food blogger. And she's *my* guest today at the food writers luncheon, so cool your jets, will you, Sara?"

"Well, how do you expect there to *be* a food writers lunch with this mess, Renato!" she shouted, and Kerry sensed the woman was on her way to a complete meltdown.

An amateur in the kitchen…

Kerry surveyed the counters. A big bundle wrapped in white butcher paper and marked SALMON FILETS had yet to be opened. Piles of winter root vegetables, including carrots, turnips and beets, along with Brussels sprouts, were draining on a sideboard—uncut. On the marbled pastry counter it appeared that Sara, her cheeks smudged with flour, had been working on making Parker House rolls. Close by, a big bag of sugar stood, unopened, probably waiting for someone to prepare the dessert.

Just then, sirens could be heard as a county fire truck and an ambulance pulled up outside. Ren dashed through the screen door.

"In here, fellas…" he shouted and within minutes, the groaning chef was strapped on a gurney and wheeled toward the door. "Sara, you go with him!" Ren ordered. "Make sure he has his wallet with his insurance information."

"But—"

"I mean it," barked Ren. "You ride in the ambulance with him and text me when the hospital can confirm what's wrong. José and I will handle the lunch. Now, get *going!*"

"Are you crazy!" she screeched. "You can't even fry eggs and José is nothing but a glorified bus boy! Send *him* in the ambulance—"

"We're going to *need* a bus boy today, and a sous chef, and a hard worker, and José is all three. Now do what I say!" he insisted.

"Or *what?*" she hissed, her eyes shifting over to Kerry. "You'll recruit Ms. CIA to replace me…after all I've done around here!"

"Will you just do what I'm asking?" Ren said measuring out his words equally.

Sara shot both Kerry and the hapless José equally poisonous glares and stormed out behind the EMT brigade. Kerry was relieved to see the woman sprint into a nearby building that looked as if it might have been a former bunkhouse and quickly emerge with a wallet in her hand. Soon, the sirens began to wail once more, and the two red vehicles disappeared up the ranch road in a cloud of dust.

Kerry glanced at her watch. It was ten o'clock in the morning.

"Well…Mr. Montisi…José," she said with a sense of excitement she hadn't felt since the meal she'd produced for her "finals" at the Culinary Institute of America, "it's two hours to Show Time. Let me lend you a hand."

For Kerry, the next hours were a complete blur as José readied the outdoor grill—located just steps from the kitchen door—and prepared the root vegetables for roasting, after which they'd be finished on the open fire, along with the salmon which would be cooked, al fresco, at the last minute.

Kerry donned a long white chef's apron that hung to her ankles and immediately went to work creating a dill aioli sauce for the salmon from a giant jar of mayonnaise, lemon, fresh garlic, Ren's olive oil, along with fresh herbs she cut from the kitchen garden when she raced out to gather a huge basket of greens for the salad.

"Be sure to mention to the tour guide that we made both the dressing and salmon sauce with Montisi Extra Virgin Olive Oil," she urged Ren with an encouraging smile, hoping to calm the near-panic atmosphere in the kitchen. For her part, she'd felt nothing but a soaring sense of exhilaration, up to her elbows in fresh ingredients.

The heart knows, doesn't it, Kerry?

Ignoring the Claddagh's latest little message, Kerry thrust a small lettuce leaf into the dressing, sampled it, and added another large dollop of Napa Valley Mustard, an additional plump garlic clove, and several more grinds of cracked pepper.

"Here…taste this," she urged her host. She dipped another piece of lettuce into the dressing, popped it into Ren's open mouth, and experienced a strange sense of intimacy in that simple gesture. "What do you think?"

Ren chewed slowly, his eyes closed. Then he opened them.

"I think it's genius." Their glances locked. "I think *you're* genius."

"Let's wait till this meal is served before you say that," she cautioned, busying herself with tidying up the cutting board so Ren wouldn't see the damnable color she could feel flooding her cheeks.

I met this man yesterday! *Cool it!*

She shifted her gaze to the ring on her right finger. The heart-shaped emerald remained green as green could be.

While the rolls were baking, the "Three Musketeers," as Kerry dubbed the efficient team of Ren, José, and herself, raced outdoors to set individual tables positioned around an open-air pavilion—designed and built to Grandmother Concetta's exact specifications, Ren explained.

"Thank God there's no wind today. We have outdoor heaters in the barn but they'd be a bitch to haul over here."

"No time, anyway," Kerry agreed. "But no worries…it's going to be a fine California day." She pointed to the thick beams supporting the building's tile roof. "How in the world did you find someone to build something so authentic? It's absolutely beautiful and completely in keeping with everything else on the ranch."

"Concetta tracked down the son of a craftsman her father-in-law knew in Tuscany and had it built in Montisi, shipped in pieces to the ranch, and reassembled here. She planted every one of the wisteria vines you see winding around each pillar."

The terracotta Italian floor tiles beneath the roof had been installed on a broad promontory overlooking olive groves that marched up and down several hills barely a football field from where they stood. A heavy basket of cutlery in her arms, Kerry paused to stare at the panorama surrounding them.

"Good heavens, this is *another* gorgeous view! And to think you grew up here." Then, she turned and abruptly asked Ren, "What did you plan for centerpieces?"

His expression went blank and he asked the question of José in Spanish, who timidly stammered, "Señorita Sara…non…"

"No worries," Kerry repeated swiftly. "You expect thirty-two guests, plus the driver and tour guide, right? Which means we should set seven tables with about five guests each, don't you think? Didn't I see some small pots of succulents on the back patio? José could wipe the pots clean, wrap them in those colorful tea towels I saw piled up in the pantry, and put them on the tables, along with pitchers of ice water with thinly-sliced lemons, and we're good to go."

"Brilliant!" Ren agreed, and translated Kerry's idea to José, who sprinted off to collect terracotta pots of local cacti, while Ren and Kerry doled out the silverware and linen napkins.

They were just putting the final touches to the table settings when Kerry suddenly exclaimed, "What was Jeremy serving for dessert?"

Ren's expression of alarm showed the anxiety he had managed, thus far, to keep under control.

"Some fruit tart thing, I think," Ren said. "Sara was up to her elbows in flour yesterday, but I didn't see anything stored in the big cooler, did you?"

By this time, José had returned with a wheelbarrow full of clay pots, so Ren inquired about the dessert course. José grimaced and answered in rapid Spanish, with doleful looks in Kerry's direction.

"José says Sara's efforts didn't quite work out so Jeremy decided this morning that he'd make pumpkin *crème brûlée,"* he announced with a groan.

Kerry fanned her right hand through the air. "Piece of cake…or I should say, piece of 'custard!' Canned or fresh pumpkin?" In response to Ren's apologetic shrug, she turned on her heel and sped toward the kitchen, shouting over her shoulder, "Never mind. This is an emergency…and I'm betting your chef said he could substitute this dessert because he knew he had ten tins of pumpkin on reserve in his pantry!"

Amazingly, all was in readiness when the sleek black Sonoma Tours buses, fresh from several stops at nearby wineries, rolled up, spilling out their occupants who were obviously feeling no pain.

"Lucky for us they're already three sheets to the wind," mumbled Ren out of the corner of his mouth as the two of them stood by to greet the arriving guests.

"Everything will be *fine*," Kerry whispered. "You play host and get them seated and their drinks filled, and I'll send out José with our *very* simple vegetable hors d'oeuvres and more wine. Then come back as soon as you can and we can get you grilling the salmon, which only will take a few minutes to cook and can be served at room temperature. Meanwhile, I'll toss the salad and start plating everything else."

Ren shot her a look of pure gratitude as he took several steps forward to extend his hand in greeting to the food writers.

"Well, hello," he addressed a large-boned woman who had been first out of the bus and sported an outsized floppy straw hat. "Welcome to the Montisi Olive Ranch. We're *so* delighted you can join us today..."

The Three Musketeers did double duty as wait staff with Kerry instructing them in her "swarm technique" whereby each guest at a table was given a plate of food before the next table was served.

"There's nothing worse than waiting for the last person to have a plate put down in front of them," she said under her breath, and then smiled prettily at the woman Ren had first greeted off the bus whom Kerry recognized as the food critic for a major newspaper back East.

Blog material alert!

She almost laughed out loud when she glanced down at the Claddagh ring glowing a shade paler than its normal emerald green.

"All right...yes, I hear you!" she muttered, sprinting back to the kitchen to line up on a serving tray three dozen ramekins of perfectly-baked pumpkin *crème brûlées* that had been cooked while their guests were having their lunch.

She picked up the device all serious chefs, including Jeremy Garafola, had in their kitchen arsenals: a mini blowtorch to perform the final touch on the desserts. She had just finished caramelizing the last crust of melted sugar when Ren burst into the kitchen, slightly breathless, with José padding into the room behind him.

"What are you, some kind of witch woman?" Ren marveled with an approving glance at the array of desserts.

"José's bussed the luncheon plates into bins we hid behind the pillars and this wild bunch are happily asking about the final course." He watched admiringly as Kerry put a dollop of freshly whipped organic cream on the top of each dessert, plus a thin sliver of mandarin orange and a sprinkle of candied ginger she'd discovered in the larder. "These are absolutely stellar," he proclaimed.

"And you can say every scrap of what we served came from the ranch or Sonoma County, yes?"

"Well, at least from Northern California. The fresh salmon were caught further north of here. The vegetables and salad came from the ranch, and the pumpkins are grown and canned in the Central Valley. So, I guess we *can* say it's all grown or produced in our state."

"Close enough for government work," Kerry replied, and handed the first heavy tray of desserts to José. "Let's rock n' roll!"

Ren picked up the second tray while Kerry led them out the kitchen door, down the brick path, and into the pavilion, her heart soaring with a sense of accomplishment.

As soon as the threesome appeared bearing the desserts, the entire assembly of food writers began to clap.

The diners were soon dipping into their *crème brûlées*. One by one, they rose from their seats and began to shout "Chef! Chef! Chef!"

From the sidelines where the Musketeers deposited their trays after serving dessert, Ren stepped forward and gave a nod of acknowledgment to Kerry, whereby Kerry nodded emphatically back at Ren—then they burst out laughing. Impulsively, she seized both Ren and José's hands, and together, she urged the three of them a few steps forward nearer their applauding guests and the trio took an impromptu bow.

The food writers' approval swelled and the kitchen staff found themselves surrounded by smiling, appreciative diners. Kerry felt her hand vibrating and was not at all surprised to hear a now familiar voice resonate in her head.

Brava! This is what it feels *like to follow your heart, Kerry, m'girl…*

The sun was beginning to sink behind one of the western hills when the last of the black wine tour busses slowly rolled across the gravel parking lot with its load of food writers and headed for San Francisco and another "dining experience" at one of the city's top restaurants. Before they'd left, Ren had given the visitors his "Grand Tour," along with bottled sample miniatures of his celebrated olive oil.

Kerry glanced at her watch and gave a little yelp.

"Oh, Jeez! I have less than an hour before my next blog deadline! Could I sit in your office and write my piece on your computer? I had no idea what time it has gotten to be."

"Of course," Ren promptly agreed. "Let me get you set up in that building over there while José and I start the cleanup. I also want to call Sara and find out what's happened with Jeremy."

"Yes, the poor guy was in the back of my mind all day," she said. "You haven't gotten a text from Sara?"

Ren pulled his cellphone out of his pocket and shook his head. "Nothing. And that's not a good sign."

"No," Kerry agreed worriedly, "it's probably not."

No sooner had Ren turned on his computer in a building next to the kitchen then they saw a taxi making its way down the ranch's entrance road. They heard the passenger door slam and Sara Lang emerged. Ren went to the screen door and called out.

"Hey, Sara! In here! I was just about to give you a call. What's the latest?"

Sara, looking weary and out-of-sorts, marched through

the door and threw herself onto a leather easy chair in the corner of Ren's Spanish-tiled office.

"God, what a day!" Then she noticed Kerry sitting at Ren's desk. "*You're* still here?"

"Kerry saved our bacon, actually," Ren intervened with annoyance. "She pitched in and we managed to pull off the lunch…quite nicely, as it turned out."

"Well, bully for both of you," Sara responded, closing her eyes and heaving a groan. "You had a lot more fun than I did, I can tell you that."

"How's Jeremy?" Ren pressed. "Did they find out what's wrong with him?"

"Gallstones. He might have to have an operation." Sara opened her eyes and looked briefly at Kerry and then back at Ren. "He said to tell you that he'd be on the phone to you tomorrow and will let me know what I need to do to keep things going. Apparently, there are a few tours of nobodies scheduled next week. Nothing I can't handle," she added with another pointed glance in Kerry's direction.

"Let's talk about this in the kitchen," Ren said. "Kerry's on deadline for her blog and needs some peace and quiet."

"Does she, now?" Sara snapped. "Well, I need a drink and then it's bedtime, don't you think? I'm completely whacked after that miserable mission you sent me on today. You owe me, big time, darling Renato."

Startled by this statement, Kerry quickly looked down at the computer keyboard and began typing the slug line that identified the name of her blog, the sequence number, and date it was due to post.

Bedtime? 'Darling Renato?' What's with that?

Jeremy's medical escort asked no details about how the luncheon went, nor offered anymore particulars about the chef's condition, but rather, stomped on ahead of the ranch manager in apparent high dungeon.

Drama queen!

As Sara and Ren left the office, Kerry turned back to the blank computer screen and forced herself by sheer habit to concentrate. Soon, she began typing furiously, relating the tale of the cooking emergency at the Montisi Olive Ranch, along with pictures she'd snapped of the plated fare she'd helped serve. She included a wide shot of the seven round tables with diners holding up their wine glasses in an impromptu salute. It had been a thrilling day, one during which she felt alive and at the top of her game. The entire experience was marred only by the heavy presence of the woman who had just arrived and made it clear she wished Ren's visitor would go away.

Kerry contemplated the blog post she'd just produced, and as an afterthought, she decided to include her recipe for the dill aioli sauce served on the salmon that had earned her kudos even before the standing ovation for the pumpkin *brûlée*. After rereading her prose to catch any typos, she pushed the Publish button and sank back in the expanse of Ren Montisi's desk chair.

She was aware of a warm, comforting sensation of being embraced by a half circle of well-worn leather that, daily, surrounded the very nice man with whom she had worked side-by-side this amazing Saturday.

Then she thought of Sara and her obvious possessiveness when it came to her employer. The situation had all the hallmarks of being quite dicey and one—given Kerry's own recent troubles as a third wheel—she wanted no part of. She wondered if she shouldn't just leave a note of thanks on Ren's desk, retreat to her rental car, and head back to San Francisco? She was bone weary herself after the day's momentous events, and, like Sara, wanted nothing more than to collapse on her 600 thread count sheets at the W Hotel.

Say goodbye in person! It's merely good manners…

With a sigh, Kerry saved her work in her Dropbox account, shut down Ren's computer, turned out the office lights, and walked up the brick path to the lighted kitchen.

Through the screen, she saw that Ren was seated in a chair next to the long wooden farmhouse table, while Sara was stretched out on the small sofa adjacent. Each had a glass of wine and appeared deep in conversation in the otherwise deserted room. The tableau looked comfortable—and familiar—as if the pair might actually be more to each other than merely employee and boss. Kerry hesitated, and then gave a light rap on the screen door.

"I'm taking off," she announced, "and just wanted to say thanks again, Ren, for the tour and our interview today."

"Weren't we going to continue the interview in my office?" he asked, swiftly rising from his straight-backed chair.

"I can email you any additional questions I have for the other blogs I'll do this week."

"You made your deadline?"

"Yep." She took a step into the room and nodded at Sara. "I hope Jeremy is better tomorrow and can avoid surgery. Please tell him I said hello." She turned to Ren. "He bought beautiful salmon. I can tell that guy is definitely an ace in the kitchen. 'Night, all."

"At least let me walk you to your car," Ren proposed quickly. "Or better yet, stay for a bit and have a glass of pinot with us."

This time, the voice in her head gave her a real start.

Say yes to the wine!

Kerry gave a small shake of her head. She was already trying to extricate herself from the gnarly threesome of Charlie, Beverly, and herself, and did not need another similar situation in her life, especially sensing the sulk that Sara had sunk into as soon as Kerry—whom she clearly considered an unwanted interloper—walked through the kitchen door.

"It's getting late, so no wine for me, thanks," she said,

trying to sound casual, "but I'd say yes to walking me to the car. I'm a city girl and—"

"Remember, the dogs and the cat keep the critters away," he said with a smile as he took her arm and escorted her out of the kitchen.

Kerry sensed hostile eyes boring into their backs as they trod the path with Prego and Scuzi following along behind. They strolled down the slight incline to the big parking lot where Kerry's economy rental had nearly disappeared in the gloom. When they reached the vehicle parked under the canopy of a palm tree sitting in an enormous planter box, Ren took the keys from her hand and clicked open the lock.

"I can never thank you adequately for what you did today," he began. "It was nothing short of a miracle that we pulled off that luncheon with such quality—and style—and it was entirely due to you."

He leaned against the car's roof, his face only inches from hers.

"No…it wasn't just me. We were the Three Musketeers, remember?"

The night sky was now studded with a million stars, thanks to the Montisi Ranch being folded into a valley far from city lights. Ren pointed out the Big and Little Dipper and the North Star as she heard the dogs patrolling along the lavender hedges nearby.

"It's so *quiet*," she whispered.

"Listen, though, and you'll begin to hear the night sounds…birds rustling…the wind through the olive trees…"

They remained absolutely still and Kerry felt Ren's tall frame radiating a heat that made her want to draw closer to stay warm against the dropping temperature. She wondered if she were imagining, too, the spark of an electric current that seemed steadily to grow stronger, compelling this near-stranger to lean down…and maybe even take her in his arms…

Startled by this thought, she turned and reached for the car door.

"What an amazing day," she said, pulling it open, an action that required Ren to take a step backward. "I loved every minute of my visit, and I really appreciated the tour of the ranch and all the good material I have for future blog posts." She cast him a sideways glance. "The one I just wrote about today went 'live' a few minutes ago. Any sharing on the Montisi Facebook page would be most welcome, especially since this will be my first blog written in California and all eyes will be watching at LifeStyleXer."

"Done!" he pronounced. "Or at least, done as soon as I get back to my office tonight." Then he added, "Where can I be in touch with you in case I have anything else to add?"

Kerry had trouble suppressing a grin while she fished out her cellphone and zapped him her contact information.

"It's probably best to text me, though," she explained. "I'll be pretty busy cranking out eleven blogs this week and following up on getting some of your guests I met today to sign on to blog about food and restaurants in their various cities." She smiled at Ren with heartfelt gratitude. "You were really great to let me recruit a few of them before they all got back on the bus. It was my only chance and—"

"Glad to be of assistance and I hope some of them pan out." He looked at her somberly. "Your new bosses have piled a lot on your plate, haven't they?"

Kerry nodded and gave a short laugh.

"They also expect me to find my own place to live within two weeks, can you believe it? After that, my room at the W Hotel is on my nickel. I've *got* to spend some time tomorrow looking for a place to rent." She found herself staring into eyes full of sympathy, a shade darker than she remembered, now that night had fallen. Flustered, she quickly murmured, "Well…never mind. It'll all work out, I guess. 'Night, now."

"Goodnight, Ms. Kerry Hannigan." He held the car door open while she settled into the driver's seat. "You'll hear from me soon," he added, and closed the door firmly.

Yes, you will…

She put the car in gear and saw that the ring offered a single wink in the murky confines of the driver's compartment. In her rear view mirror, Ren remained standing in the parking lot, his two dogs at his side, as she nosed her rented vehicle down the dirt road away from the ranch buildings. A sliver of a new moon in the December sky rose above Sonoma County's rolling hills as she cautiously found her way down the country road to Highway 101 and headed south, traveling the 39 miles toward San Francisco.

And despite the triumph of this day and the sense of wonder at the beauty of the Montisi Olive Ranch—to say nothing of the warmth in her host's manner just now—her main memory of the last ten minutes was the malevolent force of Sara Lang's parting glance.

Chapter Five

By Sunday noon, Kerry could see that her first blog, illustrated with a few of the photos she'd taken between tossing the salad and helping Ren and José serve the tables of food writers, was an instant hit. The analytics told her that the story of the near-disaster was being tweeted and re-tweeted by some of the attending food writers themselves, and shared all over the blogosphere's top food sites. And before she could even finish her coffee and eggs benedict that she'd had sent up from room service, the CEO of LifeStyleXer, Harry Chapman—Beverly Silverstein's boss—had sent her a priority email.

Welcome aboard, Kerry, and great first post! Just the right "You are there" tone we're looking for.

She was even more gratified to note that Chapman had copied Beverly, Charlie, and even the HR head, along with the little czarina, Tiffany Gergus, who had assigned her to her cubicle and treated her like dirt.

Kerry swiftly hit "Reply All" and responded.

Thanks. More to come!

A cascade of complimentary me-too atta-girls followed from each of Chapman's addressees, to which Kerry responded aloud in her hotel room, "Yeah...*right.* I bet you're all deliriously happy for me!"

As soon as room service removed her breakfast cart,

she got down to writing two more blogs based on her journey to Amphora Nueva and reminded her readers to look for the harvest date on olive oil, rather than the bottling or 'use by' date. Within another hour, she'd also produced an 800-word riff on the best winter vegetables for soup making and ideas for planting, come spring, an all-organic kitchen garden—including pictures she'd snapped with the excellent lens on her cellphone.

Just as she'd embedded the last image, scheduled the day and time for the next post—12:01 a.m. and 12:01 p.m.—and pushed Publish, her cellphone rang.

"Kerry? Good morning! Just checking up on you to see if you survived your baptism by fire yesterday. It's Ren. Renato Montisi."

As if she hadn't instantly recognized his deep voice.

"H-hey there," she stammered. "Have you heard any more news about your chef?"

"I went and picked him up from Marin General this morning. He definitely has a problem with his gallbladder and it looks as if he's scheduled for surgery in a couple of weeks…or sooner, if he has another attack."

"Oh, poor guy," she sympathized. "That's certainly nothing to look forward to."

"Look, Kerry…I'm driving into the city this afternoon to visit my grandmother at the San Francisco Towers where she's living now. Can I take you to an early dinner afterward?"

Kerry glanced at the few apartment vacancy ads she'd pulled up on her laptop computer and sighed.

"How early? I've managed to get my blog posts done for tomorrow, but I absolutely *have* to go see some apartments for rent before I find myself homeless in two weeks. I can't believe how expensive it is to rent even studios around here!"

"It's the digital explosion," Ren commiserated. "The world is moving to San Francisco to be part of this revolution and we're a small, cramped city. Why don't you text me where you'll be around five and I'll come collect you. We can eat after that."

Kerry agreed to Ren's proposal with a profound sense of gratitude that she had something to look forward to after undoubtedly chasing all over town in search of a hovel that probably would cost three thousand dollars a month to rent.

"That sounds great. I'd love to."

Then she suddenly wondered what Sara Lang would think of this plan?

It's none of her business!

Startled, Kerry didn't even try to guess where *that* thought came from. She confirmed her supposition by looking down at the glowing gemstone on her right ring finger. Meanwhile, Ren reminded her of his cellphone number and Kerry was soon in the hotel elevator, on her way to seek a new home.

Just before five o'clock, Kerry wearily leaned against a run-down wooden building on the edge of San Francisco's Chinatown district, wondering if she could face looking at yet another doghouse for which its owners were asking the moon. She texted Ren the address of her final day's attempt to put a roof over her head, and got a reply that he'd be there in less than ten minutes.

The "studio with a view" was three flights up and might have actually been a butler's pantry or very large broom closet in another incarnation. The kitchen consisted of a shelf, half-refrigerator, toaster oven, miniature microwave, and tiny sink. The "view" was of the tops of trees planted in the minuscule backyard of the neighboring dilapidated four-story building across the way.

She was just about to bid a hurried farewell to the

bored real estate agent glued to his cellphone when she heard steps on the outside stairs.

"Ah...there you are!"

Ren, appearing in the open doorway far more refreshed than she felt, was dressed in gray slacks and a cream and black Harris Tweed sports jacket.

"Perfect timing," she said, trying to hide the discouragement that had, after such a demoralizing afternoon, invaded her very bones.

Ren gave the cramped living space the once-over and said with a straight face, "Not quite right for you, is it?" He seized her by the hand and headed for the one and only door.

Kerry waved at the real estate agent, who didn't even bother to look up.

"Thanks for showing this," she called to him, "but I work at home and I'll need—"

"No worries," the agent cut in, clicking off his cellphone. "I think I rented it already." He patted a file folder. "I got five applications this afternoon. The owner is bound to accept one of 'em."

Kerry remained silent until she climbed into the passenger seat of what Ren quickly disclosed was his "city car from another life," a late-model Mercedes. He soon was headed down California Street toward the Bay Bridge side of town.

"The money around here puts New York City to shame," she groused, and then shot Ren an apologetic look. "I don't mean *you*...I could see how hard you work at that ranch. I just mean..."

"I understand what you're saying," he sympathized. "All the millionaires manufactured every time a Facebook or Twitter or LinkedIn sells its stock to the public means that twenty-two-year-olds will be outbidding you at just about every turn. It's why I jumped at the chance to bail out of being a venture capital guy and moved back to the ranch to help out my grandmother. It was all getting a bit much for my taste."

"Speaking of your grandmother," Kerry asked, "how was she? I take it she lives in a retirement home here in the city?"

Ren nodded. "A very *nice* retirement home. The San Francisco Towers is a stone's throw from the Opera House and City Hall. It looks more like a Four Seasons Hotel than an old folks home. Last month, Concetta had her ninety-first birthday, and today she was her usual peppery self, always complaining that they rarely serve real Italian food…but we had a nice lunch there together."

"Oh, you've just eaten?" Kerry asked. "Well, then, don't feel you have to—"

"I had a small salad, which is why Concetta was giving me grief. Actually, I'm starving," he said as he pulled up to the curb and gave his keys to the parking valet. "Come…I'm taking you to one of my favorite restaurants."

By this time, they had arrived on Mission Street, near the waterfront. Ren took her arm and guided her in the direction of a brass and glass revolving door. To its left was an equally shiny brass plaque that declared they had arrived at "Boulevard."

Kerry had read volumes about this eatery of renown, housed in a landmark building on the historic Embarcadero that faced the Bay Bridge whose massive silver struts soared above their heads. She smiled at Ren as they entered, delighted this had been his choice.

"Boulevard was practically Number One on my list to try as soon as I got here."

After giving their waiter their wine order, perusing the extensive menu, and then ordering their selections, Ren gazed across the small table at his diner partner.

"So tell me," he asked. "You said you were a city girl. How do you feel about living in *this* one, now that you're here?"

Unable to conceal her discouragement, given all the events of the past seventy-two hours, Kerry responded with a small shrug and suppressed a sigh.

"It's too soon to judge, I guess," she temporized. "It's just all the *pressure,* you know? The move three thousand miles across the country. The extra blogs I stupidly agreed to produce, along with all those writers I'm supposed to recruit. And then there's finding a place to live in a no-vacancy town. All that, plus a few other things I'd rather not think about."

"Tell me," Ren urged.

"Tell you about the things I'd rather not think about?"

"The reason I'm prying is that Jeremy is on strict bed rest until all the tests come back and they know whether he'll need surgery. He can only get up to go to the bathroom."

"Oh, lord…that's not good. Do you have a lot scheduled at the ranch next week?"

Her mind had started to race. She suspected Ren had an ulterior motive in mind when he asked her to dinner—other than merely wanting to connect with her winning personality, she thought wryly.

"We have a couple of no-sweat events scheduled in the next few days," he said with a shrug. "Nothing like what we faced yesterday." Then he raised his wine glass.

"Here's to you and the incredible job you did, not only saving the Montisi Olive Ranch from a complete disaster, but pulling together a meal that was truly incredible."

"Your chef had already planned it and laid in all the food—"

"Yes, but everything would have fallen apart if you hadn't picked the right stuff from the kitchen garden for the salad and made that killer dressing, to say nothing of that amazing dill sauce for the salmon, *and* produced thirty-six incredible pumpkin *crème brûlées* out of the back of our pantry. Not only *that,*" he added, setting his wine glass on the table and gently seizing her hand, "you whipped out a wonderful blog that brought the entire culinary emergency to vibrant life. You are one talented lady, Kerry Hannigan."

Ren was staring directly into her eyes as waves of palpitations in the hand he was holding out-vibrated her other hand wearing the Claddagh ring.

Perhaps there was more to his dinner invitation than pure business, she thought hopefully.

"Thank you for such kind words, but really—"

"*Really,* Kerry," he came back at her, "why do you underestimate yourself so much?"

Yes, why do *you?*

Kerry felt like slapping her right hand with her left, but couldn't because Ren still encased her palm in his own.

She affected a shrug. "I'm sure Sara could have managed just as—"

"Sara would have made an entire mess of everything," he cut in, not letting go of her hand. "In fact, she was well on her way to doing just that when Jeremy doubled over Saturday morning."

"Then why does she work in the kitchen?" Kerry asked bluntly.

Ren broke their glance and released her hand.

"That's something *I'd* rather not think about…at least not at the moment."

"Ren! C'mon! You've asked *me* to tell all. I want to know why such a disagreeable woman is in your employ…or is it something personal?" she added, and then instantly regretted such inquisitiveness on her part.

Just at that moment, the waiter arrived with their entrees and the diversion appeared a welcome delay to Ren's having to answer her question.

When at length they were alone again, Kerry's dinner companion would only say, "Sara was given work at the ranch as a result of a tragic circumstance in her family. It seemed a temporary solution that's now dragged on far too long. After her behavior these past weeks, even before you witnessed her rudeness for yourself, I've been wracking my brains for how to…how to—"

"Tell her it's time to move on?" Kerry interrupted. "It's actually probably kinder to let her know sooner, rather than later, if that's what you want," she declared, wondering why men so often withdrew their affections long *before* they leveled with the women in their lives as to how they really felt about them?

What was Ren's relationship with Sara, anyway, she wondered, recalling the sense of familiarity that appeared to exist between them when she'd entered the kitchen the previous evening. Was this a "Charlie Move?" Was Ren trying to solve two problems at the same time: unloading *his* girlfriend while acquiring a temporary chef? Because that's what all his praise appeared to be leading up to.

In the space of an instant, the atmosphere between them had grown heavy and uncomfortable. For the next half hour while they ate their meal, she strove to keep her end of the conversation light and impersonal with comments about the food and questions as to the probable source of various local ingredients. As soon as the coffee was served, Kerry pointedly looked at her watch.

"Well, this has been lovely," she said, "but I'd better get back to the hotel. Cube-land awaits tomorrow, bright and early."

Ren swiftly caught the attention of their waiter and signaled for the check.

"Kerry…" he began. "Something happened just now, and I want you to tell me what it is."

She hesitated and then blurted, "Look, you have things you must be dealing with that I know nothing about, and the same is true with me."

Ren paused. Then he nodded agreement. "That's a fair assessment, I'd say…but even so, a chill just wafted through here. What happened?"

"Since you asked, you should probably know there's a lot about my move to San Francisco that—"

The waiter interrupted with the check just then and Ren paused to sign the credit card receipt. Kerry took that as a signal to rise from her seat, threading her way through the restaurant with her escort following along behind. Once in Ren's car, she turned and offered a tight smile.

"Thanks again for dinner. It was delicious."

"We discussed the food, but didn't particularly savor it," Ren countered. "You haven't answered my question. Why did you shut down on me?"

Kerry was caught off guard by Ren's refusal to pretend their dinner date was a casual affair that had simply fizzled between two people who barely knew each other. Feeling the heat of his steady glance, she hesitated for a moment and felt a pulse of energy shoot up her arm.

"Here's the deal: on the flight coming out here Friday, I broke up with my live-in boyfriend and business partner of over a year because I found out he was having a Facebook—and now a real life—affair with his former high school girlfriend who just happens to be our *new* boss at LifeStyleXer. I'm afraid I have a lot on my mind right now."

"Good God!"

Kerry said crossly, "Well, *you* appear to have a tangled situation of your own, so…"

She couldn't think how to finish her sentence. After all, she'd just *met* the man who was now piloting his Mercedes up California Street, away from the downtown W Hotel.

Ren stared straight ahead, driving in silence a few minutes more until, at length, he said, "I am not involved with Sara Lang on any level that I think you're assuming I might be."

Why did Kerry get the sense that—as with President Clinton's denial of his relationship with Monica

Lewinsky—Ren had parsed his last sentence *very* carefully?

She was about to respond when he continued, "I'd still like to discuss one of the other reasons I asked you to dinner, besides wanting to thank you for yesterday. Will you have a quick nightcap with me at the Top of the Mark? I wouldn't be a good ambassador to San Francisco if I didn't show you the view." She could feel him studying her profile when he added, "Please, Kerry."

Ren continued to drive the car up California Street's steep incline, past Powell. She gave a brief nod of assent, then saw that right beside them, an iconic San Francisco cable car was creaking up the hill.

"It's amazing those old things are still running," she commented, hoping to lighten the heavy atmosphere in the car.

"Those babies are more than a hundred and forty years old, but they draw a lot of tourists to this town, so somehow the city engineers keep them going."

Wisps of fog had begun to swirl around the hood of their car as it crested Nob Hill, a summit that featured a square park surrounded by a group of magnificent buildings. On Kerry's right stood the six-story "wedding cake" beaux-arts Fairmont Hotel.

"It was restored after the disastrous earthquake and firestorm of 1906," Ren explained, his tone acquiring the *politesse* of a tour guide. On the north side of the park he pointed out the former Flood mansion—a brownstone that now served as the exclusive Pacific Union Club.

"Still only male members, I read somewhere," Kerry said.

"Right. Some of us have been trying to change that, but so far…no go."

On their left was the much taller Mark Hopkins Hotel. Below, Ren pointed to the Stanford Court, and in the other direction, near the towering Grace Cathedral, the Huntington Hotel.

"Some of these hotels on Nob Hill replaced the mansions destroyed in the quake that had belonged to the four railroad barons that built the western section of the transcontinental route…and so these post-quake buildings were named in their honor."

Ren wheeled the car into the gated and bricked courtyard of the Mark Hopkins and immediately liveried doormen on both sides assisted them out of their vehicle.

Kerry began to shiver in the damp, cold air. She wrapped her arms around her upper body, hurrying toward the hotel's entrance. Ren quickly caught up with her and put a protective arm around her shoulders clad in a thin sweater.

"First lesson in San Francisco. Whatever the season, always carry a fleece jacket," he joked, and Kerry could feel herself smiling in spite of the dark mood that had overtaken her at dinner.

Ren guided her up the red-carpeted steps, through the revolving glass door, and into the warmth of the plush lobby. Kerry was surprised when he kept his arm around her, even as they waited for the elevator which, when it arrived, whisked them nineteen floors to the hotel's former penthouse, now a bar with reputedly the best view of both bridges in the entire city.

Stepping out onto the top floor, Kerry halted in her tracks.

"What a shame. Look at how thick the fog is up here. There's absolutely *no* view."

"Good," Ren declared. "We have to talk. You'll see the view another day. Come…shall we take that table in the corner?"

A waiter across the empty room gestured they could sit anywhere they liked.

"A stinger?" Ren asked her when a member of the staff came swiftly to their side, since they were virtually the only customers.

"Fine," she said with a nod, wondering why Ren couldn't have said whatever he had to say to her in the car on the way back to her hotel.

"Two stingers," he repeated to their waiter who left to fetch drinks made of brandy and *crème de menthe.* Ren fingered the corner of his cocktail napkin and then abruptly declared, "I still wish you'd tell me why things went sideways with us back there at Boulevard, but since you don't seem to want to talk any more about it, I might as well just say what's on *my* mind: I want you to come work at the ranch. Starting tomorrow."

"*What?*"

Kerry seriously doubted she'd actually heard Renato Montisi correctly. Had he just offered her the job of her dreams?

"Come work for me. *With* me," he amended

"But I only started my new job out here on Friday!"

"I know that," he said with a laugh. "But *my* job offer includes full-time housing," he added with a sly smile, watching her reaction. "A cottage of your own on the property…and a few other nice perks like healthcare. Bonuses, too, if we do well."

And any other additions you had in mind?

Kerry knew that thought had *not* come from the Claddagh and felt heat flood her cheeks.

"But if Jeremy is sick, you need a full-time chef, won't you, and I just signed this iron-clad contract and—"

"The Montisi Olive Ranch needs a lot more than a cook," he replied tersely. "I need an ace director of marketing and public relations, to say nothing of better content and digital management on our website and—most importantly—a product development person if we're to survive as a small, artisanal producer. I saw from your old website, you didn't just write a blog. I need someone to do a lot of the kind of work you did for the company you sold to LifeStyleXer."

"That's only because we were a four-person start-up! All of us did *everything*, including making the coffee."

"Well, we're a small enterprise as well, and your experience in your start-up, along with all the other things you can do, makes you the perfect person for the job."

"But I've lived in a city all my life! I know nothing about ranching."

"We have to make *more* than just olive oil, Kerry, or the Montisi Ranch can't continue. We need to develop other products using the remnants left after the olives' first pressing and market and distribute them, just as you would with any item made in New York or New Jersey," he declared. "We also have to figure out ways to get more people to *pay* to visit the ranch. I think a compelling Internet presence like you developed for your own website is how we could do that."

"But Ren—"

"You are one of those rare people that knows tech stuff *and* the specialty food world *and* how to drive traffic to our Internet business selling whatever the heck we figure out to do besides just making olive oil." He flashed her his killer grin. "*And* you're a great cook."

"And you think *I* can do all that?"

"There you go…underestimating yourself, again. Absolutely I think you can do it…and *more*. Even more to the point, I think it's work you would *love*!"

Kerry frowned as she allowed Ren's words to sink in. When she didn't answer him, he ran his fingers distractedly through his dark blond mane.

"Besides all your knowledge of the food world, you have style. You can turn on a dime. You're flexible…a team player…fun to be around…considerate of your underlings—"

Kerry felt a wash of pleasure hearing such kind words. Except for her godmother, it had been a long time since she'd been offered praise like this. She suddenly thought of

Angelica with a pang of longing. If only she could hop a cab and spend some time in her wise, comforting presence discussing what happened with Charlie and, now, these new complications in her life….

Just then, their waiter appeared with their drinks and she paused until he had departed. Then she shook her head.

"Look, Ren, I can't tell you how flattered I am by your proposal, but I signed a deal with the company I moved out here to work for, and they think my blog is part of their value now, especially as they tee up their public offering. They'll *never* let me out of my contract so quickly."

Now it was Ren's turn to remain silent. Kerry wondered what else he could possibly come up with that could surmount the many impediments confronting the possibility of her becoming part of the team at the ranch.

At length he said, "Maybe there's a compromise here. Maybe you can keep up the blogging part of your current job—which is your principal value to them, right? In fact, doing that would probably only *benefit* us at the ranch, too. You could work mostly from Petaluma, and persuade the CEO to assign someone else the management of the other bloggers recruited for the ten cities." He paused and his smile was faintly calculating. "Your old boyfriend might be just the candidate for that job. Make him work for those stock options, for God's sake."

Kerry couldn't help but laugh. Then she grew somber.

"But there's one big problem with your scheme. The HR witch says no WAH."

"HR?" Ren said, his tone communicating his disdain. "Those people would be prison guards if they hadn't gotten jobs in the digital industry. You've only been dealing with the bean counters. You're *good,*" he said urgently. "*More* than good. You're spectacular in all that you do. Top brass really don't care anymore *where* you do your work as long it's as first-rate as yours is. I can speak from experience on this. Ask for what you *want* from them and you might be surprised what the CEO will say. Meanwhile, what I'm offering is a job where *all* your many talents would be put to good use!"

"You sound like an executive recruiter, not a rancher."

Ren's intense scrutiny felt as if she was suddenly minus every stitch of clothing.

"I know what I want and I'll do everything I can to get it."

"And you've decided you want me? On your payroll, I mean," she amended, "after seeing me work at your ranch only one day?"

"In a word, yes. I can't believe I've just met the one person exactly suited to help me figure out other events and activities at the ranch that people would pay for to keep this hundred-year-old place afloat."

"But, Ren—"

He didn't even let her finish her sentence.

"Look, Kerry…let me say to you what I told my grandmother today: if we can't figure out how to make this ranch pay its way, we'll have to consider selling most of the land before she passes—or she'll have to move out of the San Francisco Towers within the year."

Kerry considered what it would be like for Angelica to have to leave her home in New York at her age. "That's terrible! Are you certain it's as dire as that?"

"After this year's harvest, I did a thorough audit," Ren said, grim-faced. "The ranch is in a cutthroat, competitive business where some of the giant olive oil producers and distributors in this country and Europe sell fraudulently labeled, unregulated products that have sat in vats for *years*. Their rock-bottom prices sold to unsuspecting customers are driving us right out of business. The expenses involved in running an honest operation *and* paying Concetta's costs in that luxurious retirement home don't add up anymore," he explained soberly. "If I can't turn the ranch into a viable enterprise—I'll have to go back to the VC business and sell the place so Concetta can remain where she is."

"Would selling the ranch to keep her at the Towers be okay with her?"

A shadow of deep sorrow invaded Ren's features. It was an expression she'd witnessed when she'd rushed to Angelica's apartment in the late afternoon on 9/11.

"The last thing that should happen is for my grandmother to be forced to move—*or* sell the ranch," Ren replied. "Either choice would probably kill her in a week."

Chapter Six

Ren's somber mood signaled to Kerry that his efforts to recruit her services had been a sort of Hail Mary pass aimed at remedying a situation that was a lot more dismal than she could have imagined yesterday when everything seemed utterly idyllic in Renato Montisi's world.

Meanwhile, her mind was spinning. On one hand, she was utterly drawn to the life she'd glimpsed at the ranch, to say nothing of the sense that a magnetic force neither she nor Ren could explain was pulling them closer by the second. Still, the sensible, *logical* part of her brain told her that the notion of forsaking LifeStyleXer, and all its potential "upside," as Charlie would surely term it, to come work for an enterprise teetering on the brink of apparent insolvency might prove to be the worst of both worlds.

No guts, no glory, Kerry m'girl!

Kerry refused to glance down at her ring. *Why* was life always so complicated, she mourned silently? So many things had piled on top of her and suddenly, it was all too much: Charlie's betrayal…the sheer self-interest and meanness of Beverly Silverstein and the HR trolls she'd had to confront…her stupidity to have signed a contract she hadn't read carefully…the loss of familiar surroundings and…most of all, the absence of Angelica's calm presence. As Maggie Doyle once said: she just didn't have the bandwidth to deal with it all! She grasped for a way to let Ren down gently.

"Your proposal is amazing and totally unexpected, but it would definitely cause an uproar where I work." She took a large sip of her stinger to buy time to *think*, acutely conscious that Ren was gazing at her with unsettling intensity.

"Is what I'm proposing something you'd *want* to do if you weren't in the situation you find yourself in at your company—and with your boyfriend?"

"Charlie Miller? *Ex* boyfriend!"

"Ex," he repeated. "And glad to hear it. But on its own merits, Kerry," he pressed, "what do you think of the idea of us working together to make the ranch self-sustaining and maybe even *profitable*?"

I would so love to do that…

There was no concealing the pure joy she'd felt cooking in that wonderful kitchen for people who cared about food as much as she did, or the satisfaction of being part of a team in a beautiful place like the Montisi Olive Ranch. But there were so many obstacles standing in the way, she thought, and they came rushing at her, one by one.

"Your offer is—in a word—wonderful," she told him frankly, "but how can it work? Don't you see, Ren? You're asking me somehow to wiggle out of a binding contract I recently signed, forfeit my big pay day after LifeStyleXer goes public, and come to work for you at an admittedly shaky enterprise—just like that?"

"Yup. Just like that." His demeanor had shifted and Kerry knew she was catching a glimpse of Renato Montisi, the hard-nosed executive. "We're grown ups now, Kerry. We get to choose what we want. We also sometimes have to make hard choices and take risks."

"Hard doesn't begin to describe what's happened to me in the last week."

Refusing to offer sympathy, Ren asked baldly, "How much will they pay you for those carrot-and-stick stock options?"

"I get half a million bucks if I hang in two years past

the IPO that's scheduled immediately after New Year's. After that, I'd get more stock, the longer I stayed…that is, if they still like what I do," she amended, thinking of the contract's clause stipulating that her supervisor could can her at any point.

"Well…" Ren considered slowly, "I didn't think recruiting you would be easy, but…wow…five hundred K, plus. They must *really* think you're one of their gold-plated assets—and they're right."

"Thank you. I never quite believed it myself."

"I can see that." Ren remained silent for a moment and Kerry could tell he was carefully considering his next words. "What if you *didn't* quit your job, but simply came to live on the ranch and helped us out as much as you could until two years are up, when you could decide if life at the ranch suits a city girl like you?"

"You'd wait that long and risk my not giving you as much of my time as you need *now* to help fix things with the business?"

"Yes, I would," he said. "I know you wouldn't stint on what you committed to do for the ranch. That's how much of a difference I think you could make in our enterprise."

"Wow," was all Kerry could manage to reply.

"I'll give you the Mercedes so you can drive back and forth to the city." At her look of astonishment, he shrugged. "I like driving the truck. You'd continue your routine as a food blogger and your other duties for LifeStyleXer…and given that you won't be paying for rent or food at the ranch—and they're paying you at least some salary to boot—I bet your company could get the W Hotel to make you a deal booking a room there two days a week. That way, you can be at the ranch Wednesdays through Sundays and only be locked up in your cubicle Mondays and Tuesdays!" he finished triumphantly.

Kerry wondered if Ren had stayed up all the previous night plotting strategy to convince her to take the job.

By this time, his signature grin had spread across his handsome features. "And here's another bonus: I promise I won't work you to death the first two years and we'd share the workload on new projects at the ranch, fifty-fifty."

"Better make it more like eighty-twenty, with you doing most of the heavy lifting for a long while," she cautioned. Then, recalling Angelica's penetrating questions before she left New York, she asked Ren, "Oh. And if I said yes to this crazy scheme of yours, what's my salary down the road?"

"Well, when we know this is going to work for both of us, I'll grant you the same amount I'll be paying myself, plus a participation position in the ranch's overall business."

"You obviously learned at the knee of *The Godfather*. You're pretty much making me an offer I can't refuse."

"That's my plan."

Kerry's excitement had gone from mere bubbles in her solar plexus to a rolling boil. It *was*, in fact, her dream job—or would be, eventually, if she and Ren could make all the moving parts work properly.

A studied risk is what this is…

Working at the Montisi Olive Ranch could certainly prove a failure, but Ren's plan had all the ingredients that—if the two of them worked hard and had some luck—could result in sublime success.

"And this agreement between us will all be in writing?" she pressed.

"Every word." He seized her hand once more, and a wave of adrenaline shot up her arm. "I witnessed you operating with tremendous grace and goodwill under terrible pressure. That was all I needed to know. *You're* the kind of person I've been praying would come along."

Kerry suddenly recalled her godmother Angelica's words about her husband Brian and their getting engaged in a week. "We just *knew*!" she'd exclaimed.

He's just speaking professionally...Kerry scolded herself, and immediately she felt another jolt skitter up her arm.

No, he's not!

When she glanced down at her hand, the heart-shaped stone was pulsing pure white. Meanwhile, Ren was pointing out the window beside them.

"Well! Will you look over there? See how fast the fog lifted. There must be strong winds out there on the Bay." He smiled at her confidently. "Before you give me your final answer, I want to show you something."

He pulled her from her chair and led her to another window facing north, swinging his right arm under her chin and around her shoulders as if they'd known each other forever. The next thing she knew, her back was pressing against his chest.

"Just look at the Golden Gate Bridge, lit up, over there," he murmured. His breath near her ear was pleasantly laced with brandy in the stinger he'd sipped. With his free left hand, he pointed at the bridge aglow against the night sky. "To me, it's one of the most beautiful sights in the world...and the road across it leads toward everything I love." Ren turned her around to face him. "Please, Kerry...I know we've known each other exactly three days and you're probably still licking your wounds about what happened to the partnership that brought you to San Francisco—"

"I'm well out of that, believe me," she murmured, feeling as if she might faint from the sensation of the two of them standing so close. "I'm still pretty stunned by everything that's happened this week."

"So am I, in a way," he confessed, pulling her against him so that her hips brushed his pelvis, sending shock waves clear through her. "After you left, yesterday, it came to me, all of a sudden, in a way I can't explain. It just seemed like our talents and sensibilities would be a perfect match for everything that's important in my life." He nodded in the direction of the glowing bridge. "Please say you'll take that road out there."

Kerry sensed that any second now, he would lean down and kiss her.

"And here I thought you were just going to offer me a job as a temporary cook," she teased, tilting her face toward his.

Ren wrapped his arms around her waist so she had nowhere to look except into his eyes that had turned the color of dark amber shaded by the blackness of the night outside. No one except her godparents had ever given her a sense of being protected like she felt in his arms. Ren cocked his head to one angle, their lips nearly touching.

"Those blue eyes of yours…your hair," he whispered. "Hannigan, you're something else, you know that?"

Kerry raised her hand to brush the backs of her fingers along the side of his cheek when a sudden, alarming thought brought her up short.

"But what about Sara?" she blurted. "How will…adding me to the crew at the ranch sit with *her*?"

Renato took a step back and remained silent for nearly the count of ten. Then, he turned away from her and stared out the window at the crystal lights twinkling in the distance.

"She won't like it," he stated flatly. "Just like she didn't like it when I married her sister."

"Sara Lang is your *sister-in-law*?" Kerry exclaimed. "Well, *that's* a little factlet you neglected to disclose!"

A mental file folder spilled out all the instances when Sara-of-the-blond-pigtails had been rude and possessive, and behaving like a jealous lover, not a grieving sister of Ren's late wife. Without so much as a glance at the Claddagh ring, she turned abruptly, marched over to their abandoned table, and grabbed her purse.

Ren was right behind her.

"Wait, Kerry! Where are you going?"

"To get a cab." She turned. "Don't you get it? I don't want any more *drama* like this in my life!"

"I told you before, my wife died! She was killed in a skiing accident."

"Really? So one sister passes away and you road-test another?" Kerry snapped, turning away to head in the direction of the elevator.

Ren seized her arm to keep her from leaving. Instead of the furious expression she expected to see, he merely looked exasperated.

"You *are* still licking those wounds over that Charlie guy, aren't you?" he said, releasing her from his grip when she turned to face him.

"Not really," she retorted. "And don't tell me you didn't notice," she added sarcastically, "that your sister-in-law has the hots for you."

"Just to be clear," Ren countered, "and in case you were still wondering, Sara and I have *never* had an intimate relationship before, during or after I married her sister."

"Well, she sure acts as if you have! Trust me, Ren, I don't need another hairball like the one I'm already dealing with, and Sara's rotten attitude toward just about *everything* has all the makings of one!"

"At least let me explain why she's on the ranch."

Kerry took a deep breath.

Hear him out, silly girl!

She sighed with resignation. "Okay. Shoot."

For a long moment, Ren gazed out the big, plate-glass window that faced the Golden Gate Bridge, its blinking red tower beacons warning off low-flying aircraft. Kerry could tell he was watching a movie she couldn't see.

"After Sandra died three…almost four years ago now, her sister, Sara, went into an emotional tailspin. To put it bluntly, she had a nervous breakdown—or close to it. Her family couldn't deal with her, so I said my sister-in-law could come live at the ranch until she got back on her feet.

She's been a total pain in the ass since the day I met her in college, but I felt sorry for her. We all did."

Kerry froze. Her experience with Charlie *had* prompted her to jump to conclusions. Sara's presence on the Montisi Ranch was an act of charity on Ren's part. She could feel color rising in her cheeks.

"Oh. Oh hell!" Kerry said, turning to face him. "Ren, I am so sorry—"

"As I said, it's been over three years since Sandra's accident. Sara's a lot more stable now, and I'm the first one who wants her to move on with her life, but—"

"How did the accident happen?"

Ren remained silent for a long moment. Then he answered, "If you come across the street with me, I'll tell you the whole sorry tale."

"Across the street?" she echoed. "Why across the street?"

"Because the bar's closing and I booked a room at the Fairmont for tonight."

Kerry frowned.

Ren quickly added, "I have a meeting with my banker first thing tomorrow. I didn't feel like driving back to the ranch tonight and turning right around to come to the city tomorrow morning. And besides, the manager is a friend. He gives me a friends and family discount."

"Oh," was all she could manage, her mind skittering toward thoughts she knew she shouldn't be having.

Ren's expression had relaxed, and a ghost of a smile appeared. He lightly placed a hand on each of her shoulders.

"If I promise to be a very good boy—which won't be easy, I might add—would you consider having a cup of coffee with me where we can talk privately? Since you may be *considering* doing business with me," he said with a wry expression, "I want to give you a brief history of the last ten years."

By the time they were midway in the crosswalk that separated the Mark Hopkins Hotel from the Fairmont crowning Nob Hill, she took his arm.

"Look…I really need to apologize for judging you as I just did a few minutes ago. All situations are not necessarily the same," she added, upset with herself that she had ever equated Ren's behavior to that of Charlie Miller's.

Ren steered her in the direction of the hotel's *porte-cochère* where a series of luxury vehicles were rolling up to the Fairmont's carpeted entrance.

"Well, thank you for that. I can certainly understand why you may be a little gun shy after what happened to you lately."

"I'll tell you the gory details about that…sometime," she offered as the two of them reached the top step. "But first, it's your turn."

"Good. I want to know everything, so I can punch the guy in the nose for you. And that Beverly woman, too."

"Another perk I get if I come to work at the ranch?"

Ren laughed and nodded at the doorman who ushered them inside. Kerry walked in first and then halted her forward progress in order to say something that had continued to weigh heavily.

"If I join your staff, you're going to have an even *bigger* problem with Sara Lang, so before you tell me whatever you plan to tell me here, I need to let you know that the unresolved situation with her makes me very leery of getting involved at your ranch professionally…or personally." She was amazed at her own frank admission that she felt the same zing between them that he obviously did. 'But!" she continued, holding up one finger before Ren could protest. "I'll definitely hear you out if you promise to put me in a cab afterwards."

Ren appeared to consider the bargain and said, finally, "Fair enough."

Kerry waited discreetly in the Fairmont's magnificent

cream-and-gold lobby while Ren checked himself into the hotel. A brochure on a side table revealed that the soaring gold-leaf pillars and impressive gilded plasterwork spoke volumes about California's first licensed woman architect, Julia Morgan, who, at a mere thirty-four-years-old, restored the burnt-out hulk in the wake of the 1906 earthquake and firestorm.

She looked up from reading just as Ren turned away from the front desk and inclined his head toward a bank of elevators several yards further on.

"This place is spectacular," she exclaimed as they rode to the fourth floor.

She felt a faintly unnerving flutter of excitement when the two of them walked down the carpeted hall to his assigned room. Within moments of entering a small, elegant suite consisting of a sitting room, with a bedroom visible through a half-opened door, he had ordered room service to bring up a *cappuccino*, a pot of tea with milk on the side, "and a plate of *biscotti*," he finished, and replaced the phone receiver in its cradle.

Ren indicated that she should sit on the brocaded love seat upholstered in a subtle gray to match the gray, silk bedspread Kerry had glimpsed through the door. He settled into an upholstered club chair nearby. He inhaled a deep breath before he began to speak.

"Twelve years ago, I met both Sara and Sandra Lang at Stanford when they were undergraduates, a year apart, and I was at the business school. I met Sara first, but was more drawn to her younger sister, Sandra, because of her athleticism and…well…a more outgoing personality."

"You mean, in contrast to Sara's gloomy-gus approach?" she couldn't resist commenting.

Ren raised an eyebrow and nodded.

"Sandra was an amazing athlete…a top tennis player in college and a fanatic skier, ready for any adventure. Looking back, I think I simply got married in 2007, a few years after Sandra graduated, because the choice seemed to be either do that, or break up. During my twenties, our close circle of college friends were getting married in rapid succession and everybody we knew just expected us to make our relationship official."

"But the trouble is, you don't really know who you are, or what you truly want in life till at least after thirty, don't you think?" Kerry said fervently. "I know *I* didn't."

"I totally agree. In my case, I had my shiny new business school degree and was about to move to Mountain View in the heart of Silicon Valley, ten miles up the road from the university, and join a VC firm—"

"Venture Capitalist, right?" she confirmed.

"Yeah…some called us Vulture Capitalists," he noted with a small grimace. "We had the heady job of investing in new companies we thought might be the next Google or Facebook. Sandra's future plans after graduating centered on playing tennis and skiing wherever there was snow, and—well—*me*."

Just then, there was a discreet knock on the door and a voice called out, "Room service!"

The waiter swiftly brought their order in on a tray and departed. Kerry stirred milk from a small pitcher into her cup of tea while Ren settled back against the chair, his cup of coffee in his hands.

"In those first years after grad school and my marriage, I was basically going along with everybody else's program," Ren continued his narrative. "I was working late nights and weekends on the deals we were doing, while Sandra and her sister spent most weekends at the Lang's family house in Squaw Valley up in Lake Tahoe."

Ren fell silent and stared into the surface of his coffee. At length he said, "Sandra and I were drifting apart, mostly due to my allowing my work to be the central focus of my life, along with her obsession in the early days of our marriage to try out for the USA Olympic Ski Team."

"Did Sara ski, too?"

"Yes, but never on the level of her younger sister. In fact, that's pretty much Sara's problem. Sandra got what Sandra wanted with ease and grace, and Sara always came in second."

"Was Sara training to try out for the Olympic Team as well?"

"They both gave it their all, but it was pretty clear that Sandra was the one that had the best shot. Sara finally gave up and got a job as a glorified administrative assistant at Lehman Brothers in San Francisco and drove up to Tahoe from the Bay Area on the weekends with me, while Sandra stayed at Squaw, training seven days a week." Ren took a sip of his coffee, swallowed, and continued.

"One winter, about four years into our marriage, I got a call that Sandra had been hurt on the slopes. Turns out that Sara had goaded her sister to ski off the cornice at the top of the mountain just as bad weather was closing in. Everything had iced over and Sandra crashed into a tree, breaking her thighbone, and had to be brought out by the ski patrol. A lot of things happened after that, and my wife ended up in a coma."

"She went into a coma as a result of a broken leg?" Kerry asked, bewildered.

"After the surgery to repair her leg, she caught one of those terrible infections in the hospital. It came on fast and galloped through her system. As her husband, I had to make the decision to pull the plug. It was pretty devastating…for Sara, especially."

"Survivor's guilt?"

Ren nodded. "In spades. After all, she'd dared Sandra to go down that run and then chickened out."

"Oh, my God…"

"Yeah, it was pretty gothic. For my grandmother and me, it felt like a rerun of my parents dying so unexpectedly in the plane crash. Sara, though, was basically a basket case and in those first weeks after Sandra's funeral, Concetta and I both worried she might…do something really terrible."

"Where were the sisters' *parents* in all this?" Kerry demanded.

"Wendell and Doris?" Ren shook his head in disgust. "The Langs are the quintessential Baby Boomers, if you know what I mean. Very 'do your own thing and don't bother us.' After Sandra died, essentially they just told Sara to suck it up and not be such a pain in the ass."

Kerry heaved a sigh. "You must think I'm a total jerk…and maybe I am, but it just looked to me as if you and Sara might be—"

"I know how it looked," Ren interrupted. "Jeremy hinted to me just the other day that he also thought Sara and I had become an item in recent months because that's the way Sara *wants* everybody to think."

"That's pretty weird…" ventured Kerry, "and must have been tough to deal with."

Ren nodded. "Sara's been problematic from day one. She apparently had set her sights on me at Stanford, and when I chose her sister, she began to invent a story in her own mind that she and I had *always* been destined to be together, which was pretty weird as time went on, given Sara was partially responsible for what happened to Sandra."

"Then, why in the world did you ever bring Sara to the *ranch*—even if you felt sorry for her?" Kerry asked, exasperated.

"She'd lost her job in the crash of 2008 when Lehman Brothers collapsed and then got laid off again right after Sandra died in 2011. Her roommates kicked her out of their apartment for not paying her share of the rent and her parents were living in France. She called one day, literally begging me to please give her a job—*any* job."

"But she's been on your ranch a couple of *years*, Ren."

There had to be more to this than he was revealing, she thought. Maybe Ren had some survivor's guilt of his own?

"To my surprise, Sara made a big effort, when she first came to the ranch, to make herself useful, especially in the kitchen. Before I came to live full-time, again, at the ranch, Jeremy was kind enough to teach her the rudiments of being a sous chef." Ren put his coffee cup down abruptly and caught Kerry's gaze. "I needed the help, frankly. The ranch's finances were a mess when I took things over, and until recently, I had no idea Sara had always had this *fantasy* in her mind about the two of us. She wants what she has always wanted: the life that Sandra had. Her psychiatrist recently called me to explain."

"Really?" Kerr asked, startled. "That shrink must have felt he had a duty to warn you. Otherwise, wouldn't patient-confidentiality prevent him from saying anything?"

Ren nodded. "Right after I talked to him—the day before I met you, incidentally—I told her parents I'd done my duty and now it was their turn to deal with their daughter."

"And?"

Ren cocked an eyebrow. "I'm waiting to hear their plan."

Kerry gazed across the narrow space that separated them. "That sounds pretty open-ended, Ren."

Frustration clouded his features. "Honestly, I've done my best to treat her as a sister, but she..." His sentence drifted off.

Kerry, recalling Sara's expression of instant dislike the minute Ren had escorted her into the ranch kitchen to meet Jeremy, asked quietly, "So...basically you're in limbo with Ms. Sara Lang?"

"I've let it ride because we're so short-handed, and now, with Jeremy down for the count..."

Kerry could sense the weight of the world pressing

down on him and without warning, the ring on her right hand began vibrating.

Think, Kerry m'girl! What would make you *happy?*

Before she could weigh her next words, she heard herself saying, "Look, Ren, I'd love to work with you as a profit-sharing partner in your olive oil adventures."

A look of both relief and joy spread across his face. "You *would*?"

"Yes!" she said firmly.

"That's wonderful!"

She raised her hand in warning.

"But for this to work for me, I couldn't move to the ranch or accept any money from you until I renegotiate my deal with LifestyleXer."

"I have no problem with that."

"Let's hope LifestyleXer doesn't have a problem, either." She smiled, hoping to reassure Ren that she was willing to go out on a limb to try to find a way to come to the ranch. "I'm excited about the idea of devising whatever else we can to sell with the Montisi brand, *plus*," she said with deliberate emphasis, "I'd absolutely *love* to be Chef Jeremy's Number 2 as soon as Sara leaves."

"Great!" Ren said with an affirmative nod. "It's *all* great."

She fixed Ren with a steady glance. "And when do you expect that will be? Sara's leaving, I mean?

Ren sobered. "I can't tell you that yet, but as soon as possible. You'll have to trust that if she creates any problems in the meantime, tell me right away and I'll take care of it."

Kerry was suddenly filled with doubt. *Could* she trust this man? What if he'd made these promises merely to solve his own problems at the ranch and wouldn't actually do what he said he would?

Studied risk, remember Kerry? This is one of them…

After a long pause, she said, "Well, thanks for

explaining everything." She gave him a measured look. "I have to be straight with the people at work that I want to change my deal, so I'll make an appointment with my CEO tomorrow and let you know how it goes."

"I know this probably feels as if you're making a very big leap of faith like the one when you decided to come to San Francisco—" he began.

"Oh, no," she assured him. "This feels very, very different." She glanced at her watch. "But, it's getting late. I'd better go." She rose and picked up her handbag off the sofa. "I'll try to get in to see the big boss at work and hope I can negotiate an exit strategy where I won't lose everything I've worked for the last two years."

Ren rose to his feet, his eyes alight. "But you've just given me a definite 'yes'—yes? You're committed to come work with me at the ranch?"

"I've given you a definite 'maybe,'" she corrected him.

Kerry could sense a subtle shift in Ren's demeanor.

"Ah…the money, is it? The stock options *carrot*? I can practically hear that conversation in your head. I've heard it often enough in my own. You'd like to keep the bird in the hand and capture the one that's just fluttering within reach."

His expression had become unreadable and Kerry knew instinctively that she'd disappointed him somehow.

"It's not *just* the money, Ren! I worked my ass off to get to where someone is offering me a half million bucks, and I have every right to try to see it through, if I can. And besides, I don't want to work at the ranch behind the back of my current employer. You wouldn't like it if I did that to *you*. I need to have a conversation with the big boss and see if I can renegotiate my deal and, by the way, *you* need to get Sara Lang off the ranchero, right, *señor*?"

Without reply, he rose and walked with her toward the door.

"How about you give me your answer tomorrow

night, Kerry, after you've met with the CEO? I've got to get someone teed up right away to give the ranch its best chance for survival, and if it's not going to be you..."

Kerry rested her hand on the hotel suite's doorknob, wondering if the electricity she'd felt flowing between them earlier was merely wishful thinking on her part. In a flash of insight she could see that Ren Montisi did not like to get *left*. And, he was also a tough businessman, and likely skilled at playing both Good Cop/Bad Cop to secure what he was after. Right now, it felt as if he were suddenly playing Bad Cop to pressure her to help solve his problems at the ranch.

Was this just another Charlie Miller move, she wondered bleakly? Worse yet, was this really her dream job, or would the presence of Sara Lang in her life turn it into another nightmare?

Kerry glanced down at the Claddagh, wishing for the first time that it would offer clear guidance. The emerald retained its normal color without a hint of iridescence.

For once in your life, just do what you *want!*

Startled, she continued to stare at her hand, expecting the ring's gemstone to change color—which it did not. Those were *her* thoughts, she marveled. With absolute clarity, she *knew* she wanted to do the kind of life's work represented by the Montisi Olive Ranch, whether Renato Montisi and she were an "item" or not. It felt so liberating to finally know what her path should be! She squared her shoulders and in her most professional manner, bid Ren farewell.

"I'll do my best to get in to see the CEO first thing tomorrow. Meanwhile, let me know if you've gotten a commitment from Sara to leave by the end of the month."

And with that, Kerry allowed Ren to say a circumspect "Good night," and put her in a cab downstairs, noting that another invasion of fog off the wide Pacific Ocean now cloaked the night sky atop Nob Hill.

Chapter Seven

Monday morning, Kerry took the elevator at LifeStyleXer directly to the floor where Harry Chapman's office was located next to the glass-enclosed conference room. It wasn't even eight a.m. yet, but instinct told her that with an IPO deadline looming, the company's CEO would be at his desk when the markets in New York opened three hours ahead of California time. She knocked at his open door, apologized for interrupting, and was bidden to take a seat.

Chapman, a trim man who looked to be in his early fifties, listened without interruption as she swiftly explained her sudden and unexpected offer to live on the Montisi Olive Ranch and—in exchange for a roof over her head—lend her talents as a part-time chef and food consultant to this enterprise.

She did her best not to lose her nerve when she saw that the CEO's features had grown grave.

Before he could respond, she hastened to add, "Finding somewhere decent to live in San Francisco in my price range is practically impossible. And, actually, I think my *not* sitting in an office cubicle all day and being part of the world I'll be writing about—as I did with the first few posts you seem to like so much—will greatly enhance the quality of my blog and keep driving traffic to the parent website. I'm happy to work in the city two days a week if you'll cover a room at the W on Mondays and Tuesdays."

She nearly winced when he raised an eyebrow at that suggestion, but plunged ahead with the proposed arrangement she hoped he'd agree to.

"Honestly, Mr. Chapman," she rushed to assure him, "working among the artisanal California food producers can only be good for *this* company. I think my living in Petaluma two-thirds of the week will be good for *both* our causes."

She held her breath, watching Chapman mull over her long speech. She wondered if she had just made the stupidest move in her life.

The CEO began to tap one end of his pen on his desk.

"Okay," he said with a final flick. "Here's what I'll agree to do: The company will cover two days a week at the W Hotel and we'll keep our arrangement with you—*minus* fifty percent of that weekly salary Ms. Silverstein agreed to pay you. I'll keep two-thirds of your stock options intact—*if* the number of page views on your blog remains as high as it is today until LifeStyleXer goes public in a few weeks and, after that time, restore them to the full five-hundred thousand dollars *if* the page views *remain* at least eighty percent of that figure, on average, for the next two years."

After only a few seconds' hesitation she said, "Fair enough," and then added with a *frisson* of trepidation, "And can this new agreement be drawn up as a separate contract from Charlie Miller's? He's really much more suited than I am to managing those ten new food bloggers I'm recruiting…and, by the way," she told Chapman parenthetically, "I already lined up four good ones at the food writers' dinner I attended at Montisi Ranch over the weekend."

"Well, that's excellent news," Chapman said, appearing pleased. "Good idea. I'll make a note to have Ms. Silverstein tell him he'll manage the national food blog team once you've recruited the remaining six."

Kerry could barely keep from grinning. "Also, Mr. Chapman, I believe that Ms. Silverstein has assigned Mr. Miller some tech projects, as well. His job, now, has very little relation to what you've hired me for, which is why I'd like my contract to be separate."

Harry Chapman paused and appeared to be considering her words carefully.

"Yes," he agreed, nodding his assent. "You and Mr. Miller are fulfilling different roles now that you're here working for us. I'll let HR know what we've decided today, and have Legal draw up your new agreement."

"That's terrific."

Chapman pointed to his computer's screen. "By the way, Ms. Hannigan, my wife is a huge fan of your blog, and has been ever since you started writing it. She made that marvelous dill sauce recipe of yours for the salmon we served Sunday night and she loved the second blog you posted this morning about what to plant in an edible, organic backyard kitchen garden." He laughed. "It's a good thing I like vegetables."

"T-that's wonderful!" Kerry stammered. "Thank you so much for telling me."

He leaned forward and tapped his pen once more on the desk. "What you've been writing about is exactly what we needed to add to the mix of what we're doing around here. In fact, it's very important to the overall approach we're taking with the company leading up to the IPO. So, good job!"

Kerry felt color infuse her cheeks at hearing such high praise and rose from her chair, anxious to depart Chapman's office before he had any second thoughts.

"Thank you so much for seeing me this morning without an appointment," she said, reaching across his desk to shake his hand. "And you have my absolute promise to work harder than ever to merit your wife's and this company's support."

Harry Chapman nodded absently and began typing notes into his computer that Kerry could only assume were the details of the new bargain they'd just struck.

"Check your email later today," he confirmed, not looking up. "You can print out, sign, and deliver the new contract directly back to me."

"Will do," Kerry said over her shoulder, exiting his office as quickly as she could before she ran into any vice presidents who might be wandering the halls.

Kerry slipped into her Aeron chair inside her cubicle, pulled out her cellphone, and texted Ren the news that her negotiations with LifeStyleXer had concluded, resulting in everything she wanted in order to be able to move to the ranch as a Montisi Olive Ranch food and marketing consultant—and "Jeremy's sous chef," she added, for good measure.

Within seconds, an electronic message popped on her screen.

Totally delighted. Pick you and luggage up at seven and take you to dinner at Poggio's in Sausalito to celebrate on the way home?

She felt a fluttering and glanced at her right hand, only to realize that the feeling of butterflies was vibrating inside her own chest.

Perfect, she texted him back. Then she realized Ren hadn't mentioned the situation with Sara. She'd ask him when he picked her up at the W later.

By close of business later that same day, Kerry received her new contract and delivered it—signed—back to Harry Chapman's desk. Just as she was leaving, she nearly groaned out loud at the sight of Beverly Silverstein briskly walking down the hall in her direction. Kerry glanced at Harry Chapman's door that she'd left ajar at his request.

"You've been meeting with Harry?" Beverly demanded with a sharp edge to her tone. "What about?"

"Just summoned for a little meet-and-greet," Kerry said with a deliberate shrug. For some reason, she was no longer intimidated by the woman and continued to walk past her. Over her shoulder she added, "Turns out, Mr. Chapman's wife is a big fan of my blog. Isn't that great?"

Before Beverly could say anything else, Kerry stepped into the elevator that would take her down to the floor where she could write a couple more blogs in her despised cubicle with the knowledge she would only be sitting in it two days a week.

At ten minutes before seven p.m., she checked out of the W Hotel and made a reservation for a single room there, every Monday and Tuesday night "for the foreseeable future," as she informed the desk clerk. Ren was waiting in the Mercedes at the entrance when she wheeled her suitcase through the doors and halted at the curb.

"Is this all you have?" he marveled.

"This is it, at least until my stuff from New York arrives," she replied. "I guess I'll have to put most of it in storage until we see how everything works out."

Ren grabbed a hold of her wheelie to store it in the trunk of his car and grinned.

"It's going to work out just fine."

"What's the latest about Sara?" she said, hesitating to get into his car.

"Tell you at dinner."

Once again, Kerry wondered if she weren't about to trade the problems of dealing with one difficult female for another. As they headed across downtown San Francisco towards the Golden Gate Bridge, she longed to ask Ren exactly what, if anything, had been decided. Then, she resolutely pushed all thoughts of the yawning unknown from her mind and gazed at the dark expanse of water on both sides of the bridge. She'd made her decision, and come what may, she'd power through it.

Once on the Marin County side, Ren took the first exit off Highway 1 and wound his way down a steep incline and into the maritime village of Sausalito. Lights winked at her from the cluster of dwellings that climbed the hills above the Bay as if they were part of a landscape in Portofino, Italy.

Ren left his car with the valet, took Kerry's arm, and guided her into Poggio's Trattoria on Bridgeway, Sausalito's principal thoroughfare. Close by was a series of piers where several luxury yachts and the ferries to San Francisco docked, along with more modest sailing craft.

"What a pretty place!" she exclaimed, pointing to several art galleries and shops they passed whose windows displayed chic clothing and all manner of handicrafts.

"It's a town of about seven thousand, full of artists and serious sailors," he explained. "Sausalito is fighting to hold on to its uniqueness against an onslaught of digital millionaires who are buying up houses here, right and left."

"I can certainly understand why they might want to live here. What an amazing waterfront town, and yet so close to the city."

Once inside Poggio's, they were led immediately to an intimate leather-clad booth whose high sides bookended a table with starched linen and a forest of stemmed glasses and handsome cutlery.

Ren ordered a plate of bruschetta and a bottle of *Veuve Clicquot.*

"Shouldn't it be *Prosecco*?" she teased, referring to an Italian sparkling wine.

"This calls for busting the budget one last time," he replied and then fell oddly silent as their waiter poured the French champagne into slender, crystal flutes.

When they were alone again, Ren raised his glass.

"To you and our new venture," he toasted her, "and I can't wait to hear how you pulled this off!"

With some pride, Kerry described her session with

CEO Harry Chapman and the fact he'd agreed to a renegotiated employment package.

"Chapman seems to be a very decent guy, and he actually *listened* when I explained what I wanted to do and why. Luckily," she said with a laugh, lifting a piece of toast with tomato, basil and drizzled olive oil from the plate that sat on the table between them, "his *wife* is a fan of my blog and he appears to listen to her, as well!"

"Sounds like you convinced him to let you keep your stock options."

"Two-thirds of them to begin with, and half my current salary, which seemed fair, since I'm not available to do much else but my blogs for them." She briefly recounted the rest of the CEO's changes to her employment package, concluding, "If I hang around past the two year period, I get more stock." She smiled, and added, "But I fully expect to be working full time at the ranch by then, so *that* won't happen."

"You are the *best*, Kerry Hannigan," Ren said, smiling back. "Not bitten by the Big Bucks Bug, are you? What a gal…"

With a shrug, she popped the bruschetta into her mouth, slowly began to chew, and closed her eyes, savoring the explosion of flavors. Then her lids flew open.

"Poggio uses your olive oil, doesn't it? This is one fabulous concoction they've just served us!"

Ren inclined his head modestly. Kerry took a deep breath. Despite her brave words about her future at the ranch, she couldn't seem to stop worrying about Sara Lang. The truth was, the woman *was* a problem for her as well as for Ren, and she wanted an idea what she would be facing by living in Petaluma.

"So tell me," she asked. "What's the latest about Sara? Did you two have a chance to talk since yesterday?"

"We did," Ren confirmed. "It wasn't a very pleasant conversation, but I got her to agree to move on within the month, whether or not she's found a new job."

Kerry supposed that was progress, if not perfection.

"One problem, though," he added.

"What?" she asked, wondering what trick Sara might be concealing up her sleeve.

"We added a dinner on Tuesday for visiting experts from the UC Davis Olive Oil Center."

"That's where they test products for purity and grade and publish their findings—to the dismay of the cheaters," Kerry confirmed, "the ones claiming extra virginity for products that are actually of a lower grade?"

"Exactly. It's a big deal, and with Jeremy forced to stay off his feet most of the day, would you be willing to take charge, with José and Sara assisting? I'll help, too," he assured her.

"And protect me if Sara suddenly decides to find a new use for the kitchen knives?" she asked, only half in jest.

"I won't leave you two alone for an instant," he assured her.

"Well, if Jeremy can give us both directions from the couch, she'll probably behave, don't you think?"

"Let us hope. You and I will just have to work on marketing and product development issues later in the week."

Kerry groaned inwardly at the thought of dealing with the quarrelsome woman under the pressured circumstances of producing a stellar meal for such an important group, but then she reminded herself that Sara would be gone in a month.

"Despite my concerns about your sister-in-law," she mused, "I might as well admit to you that hanging out in the kitchen is the part of the job I most look forward to."

"Slaving over a hot stove?" he asked skeptically. "Some kind of feminist writer *you* are."

"It's pure heaven to me!" she assured him, laughing.

"I'm excited about the other things you want me to do, and I don't want Jeremy to think I'm trying to replace him, but I just love that commercial kitchen of yours, and the vegetable garden right outside, to say nothing of the wonderful outdoor oven you've built. It's just that—" She paused, gathering her thoughts. "It's just that it's the perfect *combination* of everything I've dreamed I wanted in my life."

Ren and Kerry locked glances and once again since meeting this man, their surroundings seemed to blur around the edges and all she could manage to do was gaze across the table as currents of unexpected elation filled her chest.

Just then, the waiter arrived with steaming plates of perfectly cooked *al dente* pasta coated with a rich lamb Ragu sauce for Ren, and another that was laden with freshly steamed mussels in a garlic-laced broth for Kerry.

The moment of intimacy was broken, but thoughts of Ren's nearness and the emotion that appeared to have passed between them lingered as she studiously focused on twirling her fork into the long threads of linguine placed before her.

Later, in the half hour it took to drive from Sausalito to the ranch, Ren outlined his strategy for the next business quarter. Before Kerry knew it, his car was turning left, past the ranch gate and down the hard-packed dirt road. Prego and Scusi bounded down the path, tails wagging wildly, as Ren collected her luggage from the trunk and led her up a gentle hill, past the large greenhouse situated twenty yards beyond the kitchen.

They approached a whitewashed, batten-board bungalow perched on the low rise, its two front windows anchored by dark green wooden flower boxes planted with squat holly bushes. Their bright red berries reminded Kerry that Christmas was a mere two weeks away. Could she sneak back to New York for two or three days and surprise

Angelica, she wondered, as she noticed that lights glowed from the inside of the cottage, warm and welcoming.

"Here we are," Ren announced, as he put a key in the lower portion of a forest green double Dutch door and pushed it open. Kerry heard the pride in his voice as he pointed out the stone fireplace, updated kitchenette, single bedroom, and a bathroom sporting a claw-and-ball tub.

"My grandmother used to come out here to paint in this little cottage." He gestured toward the windows. "She said it has the kind of daylight that inspires creativity…so I thought it might be just the place for a writer. José spent all day getting it ready, and I got the tech guy out to install a router so you can have Wi-Fi up here."

"Oh…that's fantastic!" Kerry replied, clapping her hands.

She followed him further into the living room where she noted the stacked logs awaiting a match to light a cozy fire. A small, round table for two took up one corner, and a hand-woven rug graced the hearth.

"What a little jewel box of a place!" she exclaimed. "And that's the perfect spot for my laptop computer," she said excitedly, pointing to the little table. "I can crank out eight-hundred words at a shot within view of gorgeous olive groves climbing up the hill!"

"So, it's not too small?"

"Oh, no…" she said on a long breath, turning in a circle. "It's perfect! This is a dream cottage for someone like me." She turned toward Ren and added gratefully, "I can't quite believe I get to live here!" As she spoke, Ren's steady gaze made her pulse speed up in dizzying fashion. "Thank you so much, Ren. I feel as if I'm in some dream…"

For a long moment, they simply stared at each other. Kerry felt in that instant that there was a strange force field drawing them inexorably closer to one another.

Finally Ren said, "I'd better go see how Jeremy is

doing." He turned away and strode toward the Dutch door whose top section was open, offering a glimpse of the greenhouse below. "He supervised José and Sara's putting together a farm-to-table dinner tonight that we served to a small group of local restaurateurs and I want to hear how he thinks it went."

He paused at the door and although the distance between them had widened, Kerry continued to sense the same magnetic pull as before. Somehow, it seemed the most natural thing in the world when he asked, "Want to come with me?"

Kerry nodded as a little ripple of happiness skittered down her spine.

When Ren pushed open the screen door to the commercial kitchen, Jeremy was sprawled on the leather couch. José stood at the sink, rinsing the last of the dishes and putting them in the heat sterilizer, while Sara was sitting at the table with a large glass of cabernet at her side.

"Hi, all. How'd it go tonight?" Ren asked.

Jeremy looked up and greeted them wearily, "Hey there…and welcome, Kerry. We sure could have used *you* tonight. It's going to be so great having you here."

Sara was staring sullenly into her glass.

"Oh? What happened?" Ren inquired.

Jeremy darted a glance at Sara and shrugged.

"I'm obviously not operating on all cylinders right now, and it just felt as if our timing was off. José was great following my instructions on making most of the food, but…" He paused and addressed Kerry. "You probably know what I'm talking about. It was one of those nights when we just weren't in the zone, you know what I mean?"

Before Kerry could respond, Sara spoke up with an unpleasant edge to her voice.

"You mean *I* wasn't in the *zone*," she mimicked. "Well, what do you expect, Jeremy? I had to do the desserts *and* make the salad *and* serve and clear—which is usually José's job!" She shot a sharp look in Kerry's direction. "Of course, you probably think that everything will magically be peachy keen, now that *you've* ridden to the rescue."

"Kerry's work the day Jeremy got sick speaks for itself," Ren said, his exasperation evident, "and you could probably learn something if you'd drop the attitude and just pay attention."

"Oh, really? *I'm* the problem? Just wait a while," Sara predicted darkly. "I googled the words 'Kerry Hannigan, chef.'" Her eyes narrowing, she pointed her index finger toward Kerry but addressed her employer. "The only paid cooking job this fraud's ever had that came up in the search results was at a sleazy pub in New York that her parents owned prior to her getting her high-and-mighty degree from the CIA." She affected an innocent shrug. "I don't get it…why is she here, Ren, unless you've got something else going on you'd like me to break to my parents who still think you're in mourning over their *other* daughter."

Ren's expression was a study in neutrality, although there was no mistaking the anger in his tone.

"Sara," he said, "I hate to *sound* like one of your parents, but you'd better just say goodnight. Then, I'd like to see you in the office at nine o'clock, sharp, *capisce*?"

Adding to the acute discomfort of everyone in the room, Sara stonily remained sitting where she was. Kerry wanted nothing more than to grab her suitcases out of the cottage on the hill and head straight back to San Francisco.

What in the world had she gotten herself into?

Uncomfortable silence continued to poison the air. At length, it was Kerry, herself, who ended it.

"Well, on that happy note, I think I'll leave you all." She addressed the exhausted-looking chef. "I've been hired here to help on the business side, but call on me, Jeremy, whenever you need a hand. I am more than happy to offer it, including tomorrow night's dinner for the UC Davis Olive Oil folks." She turned to face Sara. "I can understand how my being hired has upset you, but I am not the enemy, and you're only hurting yourself by behaving like this."

And before anyone in the kitchen could say another word, Kerry was out the door and sprinting toward her little bungalow, its two windows glowing a warm welcome in the absolute stillness of the surrounding hills.

By the time Kerry reached her new front step, she heard the kitchen door down the hill open and slam shut and two angry, but indistinguishable voices floated on the evening air. She turned around in time to see Ren and Sara gesticulating at each other and walking swiftly along the lower path in the direction of the ranch office.

Ren had probably reached his limit and Kerry wondered what he would—or could—do to resolve the situation any sooner than scheduled. She could only pray that eventually things would settle down and she could begin what she hoped was a completely new chapter in a wonderful lifestyle that had somehow fallen into her lap.

She turned her back on the drama unfolding in Ren's office and entered her new living quarters. Within minutes, she had unzipped her suitcase and hung her clothes in the bedroom closet. Her next task was to crank out two more blog assignments, which she did over the next hour and a half, despite her thoughts occasionally wandering down the hill. She'd brushed her teeth and was about to get ready for bed when she heard a knock on the door. Ren, himself, stood on the cement front step with a grim expression, his hands in his jeans pockets.

"That was bad," he said without preamble. "I told her after you left that she has two weeks to find herself another place to live. Then I called her parents in her presence and asked them to alert Sara's shrink and make arrangements to house their daughter as soon as they can. I've had it."

"But what about poor Jeremy? José's been great,

but—"

"Plan B," Ren cut in. "Like you said, you'll be Jeremy's backup, if that's okay with you, and the marketing side of things will definitely have to wait, because I fully understand that your first priority is pumping out those blogs and there won't be time—"

"As of today," she interrupted him, "my first priority is *all* of it." She was buoyed by the fact that Ren hadn't hesitated to make such a tough decision. "And we wouldn't be able to make progress with *any* of the things you want to do around here unless you ordered Sara Lang to go her merry way, as you just did." She reached out and briefly touched his arm. "I realize that there are probably many layers to all of this that I can't possibly know about, but I truly appreciate what you just did. Keep the faith, Ren," she added, echoing the Claddagh's earlier message. "We'll figure all this out."

"Well, all I can say to that is, thank God I made that delivery to Amphora Nueva in Berkeley last Friday." Without warning, he reached across the threshold and took her into his arms, pulling her close. "Otherwise," he whispered against her ear, "I might never have met you, and then where would I be?"

Kerry marveled at how natural it felt to be enveloped in Ren's embrace and she leaned into his torso, luxuriating in the mere feel of her cheek resting against his broad chest. At length, she pulled away and tilted her head to be able to look at him.

"If we *hadn't* met last week, you'd be in a lot less complicated situation than you're in right now," she chided. "But since we can't turn back the clock, how about you step into my parlor and we close the door so that every ranch hand on the place doesn't have such a grandstand view?"

Ren didn't break his hold of her, but simply moved the two of them a few feet past the front door and pushed it closed with his foot. His hands then framed her face, his fingers threading through her hair, sending cascading warmth up and down her neck.

"I have wanted to kiss you from that first day I watched you close your eyes and run your tongue over that cube of French bread soaked in my olive oil."

"Good food is a sensual experience, don't you think," she whispered, "just like—"

"Oh…yes…" he murmured, stopping their exchange as he settled his mouth on hers. "Just like sex."

His lips were soft, then insistent, then demanding, and Kerry suddenly wondered if she'd crossed some desert landscape in the past week to find a cool, comforting oasis where she could drink her fill. His arousal pressed against her midsection, signaling that the magnetic pull she was certain they'd both been sensing since the day they met had finally culminated in electrifying sensations coursing through every cell in her body.

When, at length, they allowed an inch of space between them, Kerry inhaled a shaky breath.

"This is pretty insane, don't you think? I haven't even slept one night on your ranch and look at us!"

"It's crazy good," he said, his voice ragged. "I've never felt this…this *need* to be so close…wanting another person to be part of my life…being with someone who makes me feel as if I *have* a life…"

"I feel it too," she replied, barely above a whisper, "but really, Ren, it hasn't even been a week since I found out about Charlie and—"

"Who *cares* about them?" He seized her by her two shoulders and looked as if he was almost angry.

"I don't care about them, either," she insisted, "but I care about what's happening to *us*. How can we know this is real? Talk about crazy!" she added with a rueful smile. "We need to slow down. We're supposed to be boss and employee, remember—"

"We're partners! I felt it that first day when Jeremy got sick and you—"

It was Kerry's turn to cup Ren's face between her hands.

"I felt it that day, too," she acknowledged, and stood on her tiptoes to kiss him briefly on the lips. "But we've only worked together *one* day. Let's take this partner business…and everything, really…in steps, or you'll scare me to death."

"Well, we can't have that…" he mumbled, pulling her toward him again and nibbling her ear. "Okay then…so…since I'm still the boss, I say—let's go in *there*," he declared, nodding his head in the direction of the bedroom.

"Ren! I'm serious! I want to savor what seems to be happening here…"

"You mean this?" he said, gently cupping one breast and strafing her stiffened nipple with his thumb through her clothing. "Or, do you mean plain old falling in love? Because I think that's definitely what's going on here."

"You do?" she whispered, wondering if she could keep her balance should he touch her other breast. "You can't be right. It's too soon."

"It's happened," he stated flatly. "At least to me, it has, and if I don't get out of here in the next five seconds, I might just drag you into Nona Concetta's spare bedroom and have my way with you on top of that quilt in there she stitched…which *would* feel pretty insane."

He leaned forward and kissed her again with a ferocity that left Kerry feeling as if she were a marked woman. Then he abruptly turned and left the cottage.

She stood at the open door, watching him stride down the hill toward the low-slung farmhouse where he worked and slept. The instant his tall figure disappeared into the gloom, she felt her ring finger pulse with warmth.

Know thy heart, indeed, Kerry m'girl…

Chapter Eight

The following morning, Kerry awoke at six with birds chattering outside her window, as if scolding the universe for the low-lying fog that enveloped the rows of olive trees outside her window. She forced herself to fire up her laptop and wrote another two blogs, one about the work of the UC Davis Olive Oil panel of experts whose mission it was to determine which oils they deemed of highest quality. The second post was about preparing a dinner for the same distinguished group later that night with ingredients that would come within a ten-mile radius.

By eight-thirty, a damp chill continued to linger in the air when she walked down the hill, her mind focused on sipping a strong cup of coffee that she hoped José had made by the time she arrived at the building housing the ranch's commercial kitchen.

She pushed open the door to an empty room and flipped the light switch to search the well-organized pantry for the coffeemaker, filters, and grinder, happy to discover a bag of San Francisco Fog coffee beans in the big walk-in freezer.

She'd scrambled a dozen eggs for whoever would eat them and perused Tuesday night's menu that Jeremy had posted on the cork bulletin board. José soon appeared, followed five minutes later by Chef Jeremy, himself. After a congenial consultation, all three got busy doing the prep for the UC Davis dinner. When Sara hadn't made an appearance by eleven o'clock, Kerry called Tony, "the Salad Associate at LifeStyleXer," she explained with a grin to Jeremy. Tony instantly said he was delighted to lend a hand as soon as he got off work at the company cafeteria.

"If we can't depend on her," Jeremy agreed, "a cook's gotta do what a cook's gotta do."

Around one o'clock Sara flounced into the kitchen with Ren—who'd been informed of her tardiness by Jeremy—following close behind. She announced pointedly to the chef that she would make the dessert and salad dressing.

Jeremy and his second-in-command exchanged looks, but Kerry kept to the task she was currently assigned without comment. Ren assumed the job of peeling a pile of root vegetables José had pulled from the garden that morning.

Out of the corner of her eye, Kerry noticed that Sara had quickly proceeded to measure out oil for the cake batter she was making. While the round pans were baking in the oven, the young woman silently poured oil from the same bottle into a bowl containing the ingredients for mustard vinaigrette.

Fifteen minutes later, Kerry smelled something burning.

"Your cakes!" she cried, and raced over to the large stainless steel commercial oven on the far side of the room. She glanced at the temperature gauge. "You set it at *five hundred degrees*, Sara!" she shouted. "What the—"

Sara merely smiled and said, "Oh. Really? Gee. Sorry. My mistake," and continued to whisk the oil into the salad dressing.

Jeremy pulled himself off the couch and moved with obvious discomfort to Kerry's side, glancing worriedly at the clock.

"Shit, Sara!"

Kerry opened the oven just as one of the cakes burst

into flame. The others were already blackened and useless. She flicked off the oven, grabbed a quilted mitt, and tossed the cake and its pan into the stainless steel sink where José turned the water on to put out the flames. Alarming hissing sounds and smoke filled the kitchen while Sara remained where she was, calmly whisking the salad dressing.

"You did this on purpose," Kerry accused her, racing to open the door and windows to prevent the smoke alarm from sounding. "You're either just a jealous idiot or a very sick puppy. You could have burned down the place!"

By this time, Jeremy and Ren had joined the two women who were less than a foot apart, glaring at each other through the smoky interior.

"I don't actually care which it is," Jeremy shouted at his erstwhile sous chef. "Just get *out* of here, Sara. Go sit in your room until your two weeks are up!" Kerry could tell that Jeremy already appeared to regret he'd jumped off the couch so quickly when the cakes caught fire.

Sara whirled to face the chef. "So Ren told you I have to leave in two weeks, instead of a month?" She was red-faced and Kerry wondered if she would, indeed, seize a butcher knife and go after anyone within reach.

"Yes," Ren confirmed. "I told him this morning."

Ignoring her employer, she shouted at the chef, "And did he tell you he's already shacking up with Ms. Perfect here?"

"It's none of my business who he's shacking up with!" Jeremy replied, his complexion drained of color. Kerry thought she saw him wince with pain.

Kerry banged her fist on the counter near the bowl of vinaigrette.

"I am *not* sleeping with the boss, though I imagine I will one of these days, Sara, so I think you have a choice: make an utter mess of everything in the time you have left here on the ranch where your brother-in-law offered you shelter and amazing kindness—or pull yourself together and grow up! But one thing is certain…you can't have your late sister, Sandra's life, and you sure as hell can't have *mine*!"

The look that passed over Sara's features was a blend of shock and pure hatred. Meanwhile, Kerry detected a highly unpleasant odor wafting from the bowl of salad dressing Sara had been making. On impulse, she grabbed a spoon and stuck it into the emulsified liquid to sample it.

"Good God!" she exploded, squeezing her eyes shut. "This salad dressing is *rancid*!" She opened her eyes to stare at Sara, the full extent of the woman's efforts to sabotage them becoming all too clear. "You deliberately used discarded oil from that back shelf in the mill that would *ruin* the Montisi Ranch's reputation with the UC Davis olive oil experts tonight when we served them a salad that would taste absolutely disgusting!"

Sara ignored Kerry's accusations and turned on Ren, instead.

"You haven't even known this woman a *week* and she swans in here and practically takes over the place."

"Sara, just stop it!" ordered Ren.

"I won't stop it!" Sara's voice had gone up an octave and she seemed on the edge of hysteria. She shook a finger at Ren, her eyes narrowing. "I know what you've got planned, installing her in your grandmother's cottage that Sandra always wanted for her workout studio! You're just waiting for Concetta to kick off and until she does, you'll keep this Hannigan woman around until her stock options reach 'bingo' in a couple of years. That should tide you over and solve your current cash-flow problems, won't it?"

"How do you know about *my* stock options?" Kerry demanded, glaring at both Sara and Ren.

Sara continued, unfazed by Kerry's outburst.

"You'll be sitting pretty, won't you, Ren? She's got a better payout potential than the Lang family, you think? Traded us in for that little bitch, have you, you bastard!"

Ren ignored Sara, urgently saying to Kerry, "I have *never* discussed your financial situation with anyone!"

It was Sara's turn to bang her fist on the counter. "You think it's beneath my dignity to listen at office doors when our future is at stake, Renato Montisi?"

"*Our* future? For God's sake, Sara, we don't *have* a future!" Ren exploded. "We've never had one—before, during, or after I met your sister. And as sorry as I am that Sandra died at such a young age—and in such a terrible way—neither of you, nor your parents, ever seemed to grasp what was important to anyone but yourselves!"

Sara was shaking with fury. "Well, I can see, now, that the only thing really important to you is this ranch…and that you'll do virtually anything to keep it afloat! Even latch on to Ms. Moneybags Hannigan, here, whom you've known about ten minutes! And you think *I'm* crazy? *You're* crazy—like a fox!"

Kerry's gaze swept the kitchen. Ren and Sara looked as if they were about to come to blows. Jeremy had collapsed on the couch and was massaging his stomach. José's face had a pinched expression, no doubt straining to better understand the heated English being shouted by his co-workers.

Oh, Lord, thought Kerry, was Ren Machiavellian enough to be waiting for his grandmother to die, meanwhile latching onto some potential 'venture capital' to keep the business going? Was all the heat generated last night manufactured because of a couple hundred thousand dollars' worth of stock options?

Her brain felt as if it were about to explode. Then a voice in her head brought her up short.

Kerry! Don't be daft. Get the facts!

Kerry shook her head as if refusing to listen to the thoughts flying through her mind and made a beeline for the door, slamming it shut with tremendous force and sprinting up the hill to the safety of her little cottage. All the way along the path she blotted out the Claddagh's cautioning voice, wondering—even if Sara was a "borderline personality" and her accusations about Ren were false—how she, Kerry, could ever achieve any sort of serenity in her life with Ren's past with the Lang family permeating everything?

What *was* this? *Fatal Attraction—Part 2*?

Exhausted by her warring thoughts, Kerry shut the Dutch door with a bang and turned the lock, her eyes filling with tears. Had she been so vulnerable last week that she had blindly walked into a situation that was either Charlie Miller all over again—or something worse?

She lowered her gaze to her right hand. The ring's clear emerald stone stared back at her coldly. Maybe she should have just toughed it out in her cubicle at LifestyleXer. At least, in two years she'd have half a million bucks coming her way and not have to deal with lunatics like Sara Lang.

So, you're going to believe the one person on this ranch who wishes you ill?

"Oh, shut up, will you?" Kerry exclaimed, shocked to see that the ring was glowing as if it were a white rose in full bloom.

Renato Montisi loves this land and its bounty in the same way you do!

Kerry clapped her hands over her ears. If she couldn't stomach Life With Sara, or the cubicle on Howard Street, or the techie creeps in all of Silicon Land—she could just chuck it all! She could simply hand over her blog's rights to Harry Chapman, go back to New York, and work at her parents' restaurant until she figured out the rest of her life.

But even if you did slink back to Manhattan, you'd never know how it might have turned out with you and Renato Montisi!

The Claddagh ring had suddenly begun to pulse like a mixed-up stoplight, alternating between an emerald gemstone and an opal. Obviously, her thoughts and the ring's were clashing and it was slowly driving her crazy.

"Will you please *stop!*" she begged aloud. "Leave me alone!"

Unbidden, a memory of Ren flashed in her head, outrageously handsome in his well-worn jeans and work shirt, leaning forward in the kitchen as she slid a lettuce leaf, dripping in the mustard dressing she'd made with the ranch's olive oil, between his lips and the intimate look of pure pleasure that had passed between them.

Remember those moments…remember what makes you happy…

"It's going to make me happy if my blogs keep driving traffic to LifestyleXer dot com and I earn half a million bucks!" she yelled into an empty cottage.

Oh, really?

Steeling herself, she sat down at her tiny kitchen table, the early afternoon sun flooding through the front windows. She knew what to do! She'd write about as many subjects as she could think of in order to bank pieces if she should decide, in fact, to throw in the towel at the ranch and move back to San Francisco to toil in her cubicle and live in some hideous apartment that doubled as a dog house. At least, that way, she could avoid being sued by Harry Chapman for breach-of-contract while she waited for two years to pass…

And what a horrible way to spend two years…

She might as well face it, she though morosely. She and the ring on her finger had painted themselves right into a corner.

Hunched over her laptop for the next hour, Kerry's back was aching. Before she shut down her computer, she made a quick check of the online metrics in the last twenty-four hours to confirm that her blog posts were still were gaining page views as they had been since the very beginning of CookChic. Then, as was her habit, she scanned the comments posted below her last several blogs, and reared back in her chair, staring in disbelief. A series of nasty remarks from visitors whose names were unfamiliar and did not include any of her usual fans formed a column of negativity the likes of which she'd never seen from the first day she began posting. Even while she was looking at the screen, four or five more popped in between a few of her stalwart supporters that had begun to reply in her defense.

"What the—?"

Every time she refreshed the page, a few more ugly comments winged in, all of them slamming either her writing or her opinions.

There could only be one answer to what was going on: Sara Lang.

That woman is a devil!

Kerry felt the ring grow warm on her finger.

That woman has a big hole in her heart that you didn't cause and you can't cure. Just do your job!

Her job? She *was* doing her job! She was writing the best material of her life and look what was happening!

Then she suddenly remembered: tonight's dinner for the visiting olive oil experts! She'd abandoned ship and it was just after four. Out her window, Tony's battered Jetta had just wheeled into the gravel parking lot and screeched to a halt.

Two hours to Show Time!

Whatever was going on in her personal life had to be put on hold. She couldn't let poor Jeremy down.

By some miracle, Jeremy, José, Tony, Ren, and Kerry produced an excellent dinner of roasted Petaluma organic chicken, marinated in this year's Montisi olive oil, garlic, fig-laced balsamic vinegar, and crushed, fresh rosemary. The poultry was plated on a bed of perfectly steamed root vegetables, fresh from the garden, along with Tony's *carpaccio* salad as a starter. Dessert consisted of tarts made with fruit from a neighboring orchard. Kerry had folded puff pastry over halved pears, along with caramelized sugar, in several of chef's large frying pans and baked them—pan, fruit, and all—in the oven.

"Wow!" said Tony admiringly as he watched Kerry invert the contents of the pans onto large, round platters, fruit-side-up and surrounded by a golden, flakey crust. "That's amazing!"

"It's a great thing to do when you're really pushed," she replied, "and fortunately, Jeremy keeps a well-stocked pantry for just such emergencies. The puff pastry is from a box, but of course, it's the *best* brand."

Kerry and Ren had exchanged barely ten words during the frenzy that preceded the dinner, and Kerry helped with the cleanup in the kitchen while he entertained his guests following the meal.

Sara was nowhere to be seen. When Tony and José went out to the pavilion to bring in the last of the dishes, Kerry asked Jeremy what had transpired after she escaped to the cottage earlier that afternoon.

"She just stormed out of the kitchen as soon as you left. Ren followed her, trying to talk some sense into the woman. No doubt our very own drama diva's still sulking in her room," Jeremy said wearily, sinking onto the couch. "And Kerry…I just wanted to say…I hope you didn't take anything she said about Ren seriously."

"Hey…" she replied, trying to keep a light tone, "this whole deal with me here on the ranch is just a shakedown cruise," wondering how many more revolting comments had been posted to her blog by now?

"Not as far as I'm concerned," Jeremy replied. "I've

decided to have my gall bladder taken out next week. I hope we can count on you to keep this boat on course."

Kerry hesitated, and then said, "Of course. I'll stay here at least until you're back on your feet. After that, frankly…it's anybody's guess."

Within the half hour, the kitchen was restored to its usual, pristine condition and Kerry walked Tony out to his car, relating to him the cascade of negative comments that had suddenly appeared in relation to her latest blog posts. She briefly described recent events at the ranch and outlined her suspicions that Sara Lang might be the cause.

"Well, let's find out if it is her," Tony said.

"Can you do that?"

"We can try. I've got a few geek buddies at work who can run a check on the names and Internet addresses of the people posting that crap." He grinned. "The NSA's got nothing on these guys. I'll text you later."

"Tonight?" Kerry asked, startled to think that she might quickly get to the bottom of what was going on.

"Tonight, or first thing tomorrow. These are the weird nerds at LifeStyleXer who sleep under their desks." He gave her a buss on the cheek. "And thanks for asking me to work tonight." He waved an envelope containing the cash she'd given him. "This ranch is da bomb!"

That night, Kerry slept fitfully, hoping to hear a ping on her cellphone that Tony had sent her a text message identifying who was piling in with so many damaging comments that could bring her page views down and—if the negative spiral continued—cause her to miss the goals the CEO had set in order for her stock ultimately to vest.

By six-thirty, dawn was just filtering through the olive groves outside her window, and still there was no word from Tony—or any text from Ren, for that matter. She decided to dress, bundling up in a turtleneck sweater and a puffy down vest and knee-length coat to ward off the early morning chill. To pass time until Tony contacted her with news, she ventured out of the cottage and along the lavender hedges that would be blooming in June, Ren had told her.

You don't want to miss that, *do you?*

She glanced down at her ring, glowing eerily white in the gloom and uttered her favorite French curse. "*Merde!*"

She snapped off a lavender stock and sniffed it, detecting the faintest essence of the familiar scent, even without a bloom. She had always adored this particular aroma, especially in those bars of lovely French soap or in body lotion…

Staring at the sage green plant held between her fingers, a jumble of thoughts began to crowd her brain.

I love this place…I love this life! *I want to learn to be a steward of land like this…to grow and make wonderful food! To find new uses for what's currently discarded. No grasping, manipulative, crazy—okay,* wounded—*woman is going to drive me off without a fight! Ren and I are exactly the same: this sort of life…this* path…*is the path we choose to walk.*

By this time, not only was her hand vibrating wildly, but her entire body was shaking, whether due to the morning chill or something Kerry found quite frightening to contemplate: she was either as off her gourd as Sara Lang, or the Claddagh ring knew her far better than she knew herself…

Then, she actually heard her stomach rumble.

She needed a cup of good, strong tea, and she needed it *now*!

Kerry once again found the kitchen deserted at this early hour and immediately flipped on the electric kettle. Then she set up the coffeemaker for the others she knew would soon be streaming in, and cracked a dozen eggs into a bowl, certain that "if she scrambled them, they will come."

Sure enough, Jeremy was the first to pad through the back door in jeans and a ranch T-shirt. He gratefully accepted a cup of proffered coffee while she sipped her tea.

"How's your midsection feeling this morning?" she asked.

"Holding its own…for the moment." He nodded at the pan of beaten eggs she was slowly stirring. "Nice simple food for this boy until I have the operation."

Next, Ralph Larimore, the head gardener, walked in, followed by José, each dishing up the eggs she'd concocted, laced with fresh thyme, along with toast and jam Jeremy had made from ranch strawberries grown the previous season.

Kerry had almost finished her breakfast when Ren strode through the screen door and served himself the last scoop of scrambled eggs.

Still standing, plate in hand, he asked Kerry to follow him to his office before reminding Jeremy that some bath and beauty products moguls were scheduled to arrive for heavy hors d'oeuvres and wine pairings from four to six, later that day.

"They're going on to have dinner up in Healdsburg and spend the night there," he explained. "We should have them here for drinks and the hors d'oeuvres only about two or three hours."

"No problem, boss," said Jeremy as Kerry followed Ren out the kitchen door.

"Beauty product moguls?" Kerry repeated. "You must be kidding! They want to visit an olive ranch instead of a winery?"

"They're doing both," he replied, his features continuing to reflect tension from the drama with Sara the previous night. "They're part of some trade group from New York and LA—here mostly for a tour of the Sonoma vineyards—but our agent booked them for a drop-by here, too. Ka-ching, ka-ching…though not very much."

By this time they'd entered Ren's office, his desk littered with spreadsheets.

"Looks like you've been working all night," she commented.

"Nearly. I wanted you to know exactly where we stand financially, and to try to convince you that everything Sara claimed was false about my waiting to pounce on your incipient millions."

"Oh, Ren…" she began.

"The trouble is," he cut her off, "as I told you before, we *are* on shaky ground, but that is *not* why I felt like hauling you off to a cave somewhere yesterday."

Kerry offered a bleak, apologetic smile before she replied. "I gave what happened in the kitchen yesterday some serious thought and concluded that Sara was just projecting what *she* would do if she thought she could get her hands on someone else's money. She reminds me a lot of Charlie Miller."

"I told her last night to clear out. Today. Even if you weren't in the picture, her last little number—using rancid olive oil in a meal for the very people who are trying to expose the crooks in our business—crosses a line that can never be erased. She's toxic and there's nothing I can do to fix her. I honestly hope she'll be okay wherever she ultimately lands, but I'm counting the minutes until she leaves."

Kerry could see that Ren was upset in a way he couldn't disguise and her heart went out to him. With everything he was dealing with, and *had* dealt with since his wife's death, Sara's betrayal had obviously struck deep. She was tempted to tell him of her suspicions regarding the vicious comments on her blog, but decided not to add to his woes until she had confirmation from Tony and his cyber-sleuths.

Instead, she said, "Well, I've got something that may cheer you up."

"What?"

"You're not going to believe this, but I have an idea you could suggest to your guests tonight—or at some point in the future."

"You do? *What?*" he repeated.

"What if *we* started a line of natural products like soap and body lotion made from the second press of the olives, *plus* our own lavender essence harvested from all those lavender plants around here? And if we can't produce enough, we can contract with other olive ranches and lavender farms in California, but brand it as our own special formula—which it will be."

Ren gazed across his desk with a look of amazement.

"Now, why couldn't *I* have thought of private label beauty products? I've been staring at those rows of lavender since I was a toddler!"

Kerry laughed and settled back in the chair opposite.

"Yeah…but I'm female and I *love* all that lavender-scented stuff like body lotion, bath oil, and bubble bath!" She smiled encouragingly. "Promise we can have bubble bath as one of our products?"

Ren leered at her across the desk. "What an arresting thought. You. Naked in a bathtub filled with Montisi's lavender bath gel."

"Not so fast, big guy! There are a few other things we need to discuss."

Ren regarded her for a moment, a distant, guarded look invading his eyes.

"Just tell me, Kerry. Are you going to stay…or go?"

She hesitated less than an instant before she answered.

"Stay."

"Even after what happened yesterday?"

"Just let me know when Sara Lang has left the building, will you please?"

Ren's expression revealed he didn't know if she was kidding or not.

"What if I offer you a fifty-fifty deal on this bath products idea—if we can make it work?"

Kerry sat straighter in her chair. "Renato Montisi, if you are suggesting that I am merely withholding my favors, just to strike a good deal—"

"Absolutely *not!*" he cut in. "I'm saying I need a partner like you…in my work…and in my *life*. If that scares you, I'm sorry…but you'll just have to accept that's how I feel."

"It does scare me a little. It's only a week on Friday since I put on—"

Ren looked puzzled at her non sequitur. "Put on what?"

She hesitated to provide an answer. Did she really know Ren well enough, yet, to talk about the ring on her finger?

"It's nearly a week since I left New York," she amended, "and met you the very same day. I can't believe I'm living here…in such a beautiful place. I can't believe…*any* of it. But here I am," she said smiling at him with a rush of happiness she couldn't deny to either of them. "It's all been pretty amazing, don't you think?"

Ren leaned forward and seized both her hands in his, a look of relief spreading across his face.

"What's even more amazing is that I feel as if I've known you, always."

Kerry nodded. "It was if we *recognized* each other the moment we met. It's absolutely crazy, isn't it? No wonder it drove Sara bonkers. She sensed our connection, right from the first."

Just at that moment, she glanced out of Ren's office window and spied his sister-in-law hauling a big suitcase across the gravel parking area. Sara yanked opened the trunk of her car and heaved in the piece of luggage, along with several other cases sitting nearby. Without a pause, she retraced her steps toward the building Kerry assumed was where she slept—and disappeared through its door.

Clearly, she was leaving the ranch.

Kerry's mobile phone pinged. It was a text message from Tony.

Call me asap

Meanwhile, Sara had reappeared with another suitcase.

"So she *is* actually leaving," Kerry said, pointing out the window. "What about her family? Has she some place to go?"

"Tahoe. Her parents grudgingly said she could stay in the house up there for a while and look for work at one of the hotels. I told her if she behaved herself for six months, I *might* write her a reference about her work here."

"You are a very decent man, Renato Montisi," Kerry said quietly. "I actually feel very sad for her, but I'm glad you're not giving her your recommendation right away."

Sara Lang was a totally confounding person, and before Kerry could detail for him what had been happening overnight on her blog, Ren said, "And, just for the record, I don't give a flying fig about your stock options. Who knows, if in two years, they'll even be worth the paper they're printed on. I've seen a few IPOs get bad press right before they've gone on sale and then tank, big time. I hope you get that dough, but a lot can happen in the tech world in that time."

Kerry's stomach clenched. What if Sara's backhanded efforts not only screwed up *her* potential payday, but also diminished or sabotaged LifestyleXer's IPO, itself?

Ren seized her hand once more, forcing her thoughts back to the present.

"Look, Kerry…who can tell what's ahead for us after only knowing each other such a short time, but I want to say here and now that I will *never, ever* ask you for a penny of your money. You and I and the rest of the crew on this ranch are going to get this place onto solid ground by dint of our joint efforts, doing projects like your brilliant idea, just now, to make olive oil and lavender-based bath and beauty products."

"But what if that idea is a bust? There might be too much competition, or we can't get the distribution, or—"

"Look! You're the one who said 'Keep the faith.' If we don't succeed at this or some other idea we think up, I can go back to being a VC and *you* can run the ranch."

Kerry had a sudden thought. "But if Concetta gets wind you've gone back to Silicon Valley…she might decide to sell this place."

"She can't."

"Of course she can!"

"She's already deeded the ranch to me. The week before last."

"She *has*?"

"Concetta's turning ninety-two this year. She and I had talked about how to arrange her affairs in her final years so she'd want for nothing. She insisted before the end of the tax year on putting me on the deed as co-owner with the right of survivorship. I told her to do it *only* on the condition I could make it pay enough to sustain her at the Towers. If I can't, then we sell the place and put the proceeds to fund her living where she is."

"Ah, yes…" Kerry said with a smile, "you told me how she's queen of the San Francisco Towers. But it's super deluxe, right?"

"Very. The Towers is practically next door to the Opera House, and she couldn't be happier—and neither could I. I have her power-of-attorney and I decided last night that I won't even tell her if I have to sell."

"You are truly a stand-up guy, Renato Montisi…especially given how hard it is to make a living as a rancher."

"Well, she raised me, remember. It's the least I could do for her at this stage of her life. If everything goes south here, I can always carve out ten acres of the eight-hundred for ourselves, build a little house on them, and suit up as a Vulture Capitalist again."

Ren paused and pointed out his office window as the two of them watched Sara prepare to get into her car. Kerry hesitated for only a moment and then told Ren about the bizarre raft of negative postings that had suddenly plagued her blog.

"Do you think I should confront Sara before she drives away?" Kerry said, rising from her chair and preparing to sprint out the door.

Both Ren and a voice echoed in her head. "No...we need to get the facts before we make a serious accusation like that."

Kerry glanced down at the phone in her lap.

"Oh, my God! I forgot! Tony just texted me. Maybe he has some news."

The cellphone only rang once before her call was answered.

"Kerry? You won't believe this." She swiftly put her phone on speaker mode so Ren could hear Tony. "My tech buddies had a hell of a time last night, but guess who they finally think were responsible for those nasty-grams?"

"Sara Lang," Kerry pronounced with a sinking heart, watching Sara's car roll across the parking lot and head down the drive.

"No!" Tony lowered his voice to a hoarse whisper. "We think it has to be Charlie Miller and Beverly Silverstein!"

Kerry could only stare, open-mouthed, at Ren whose expression told her he wasn't particularly surprised to hear this.

Tony continued, "My guys traced most of the IP

addresses back to LifeStyleXer, though the names of the supposed commentators are all bogus."

"Then how can we prove it's Charlie and Beverly?"

"Well here's the weird thing. Both of them posted some *positive* comments from their own email addresses at the company...probably to cover their tracks. With Beverly's supposedly *nice* posts, she used the Safari browser to access the Internet...but Miller apparently posted *both* his real and a few of his bogus comments using an obscure browser called 'Bark.'"

"You mean he didn't use Chrome or Safari?" Ren cut in.

"Right. The nice comments he made under his own name, *and* some of the nasty ones you saw on your site, *both* were posted via the *same*, weird browser, Bark," he reiterated.

Kerry turned to Ren. "Bark was founded by a fellow tech pal of Charlie's. It's never really caught on. He's the only person I know who still uses it."

Tony chimed in, "It's just circumstantial evidence, but it's pretty strong."

"As they say in the crime shows," Ren commented dryly, "both those two had 'motive, means, and opportunity,' plus—apparently—Bark."

Tony said, "I had the guys make printouts of what they'd tracked back to Bark, but get your fanny back to town. This is pretty explosive stuff, and I don't want any of us to get nicked by the shrapnel."

"We'll be there within the hour," Ren announced. To Kerry he said, "C'mon...let's go! I'll ride shotgun."

Kerry nodded, jumping up from her chair. To Tony on her cellphone she said, "You are way more than Salad Man, Mr. Perez...and trust me, I won't forget this."

"How about someday making me a sous chef to your sous chef, as long as it's not working with that nut job I met yesterday."

Kerry glanced out of the window just as Sara Lang's car disappeared from view.

"No worries on that score," she said, pointing silently out the window for Ren's benefit. "In fact, we need to bring you back with us to help with a bunch of bath and beauty products tycoons visiting the ranch late this afternoon. See you soon, and *please*…put those printouts somewhere safe, will you? Meet you in the cafeteria."

Chapter Nine

Forty-five minutes later, Ren nosed the Mercedes into a parking spot in the subterranean garage of LifestyleXer's office building on Howard Street. He and Kerry sprinted toward the elevators that would take them to the company cafeteria. They froze at the door. Beverly and Charlie were sitting together in front of a laptop at a table for two at the far side of the large room.

"Looks like they're still at it," Ren said in a low, angry voice. He whipped out his cellphone and snapped a picture of them huddled over the portable computer, instant messaging the image to Kerry's phone.

"Yeah, busy trying to torpedo yours truly, her blog posts, and—ultimately—her payday," she whispered back.

Fortunately, the pair was so absorbed in what they were doing that they never looked up. Behind his salad-making station, Tony glanced in both directions before he handed Kerry a file folder.

"It's all in there," he said in a hoarse whisper, handing her the evidence that Kerry clutched to her bosom.

"Let's get out of here before they see us!" Ren urged, and soon the two were back in the elevator riding up to the CEO's floor.

When they arrived at Harry Chapman's office, his administrative assistant's chair was empty but, fortunately, Kerry's boss was at his desk, a plate with a sandwich and potato chips sitting beside his computer screen. Ren waited just outside the door as Kerry gave a quick knock and apologized for the interruption. As succinctly as she could, she described what had been happening to her blog posts.

Chapman's expression grew grave as he studied the printout detailing the raft of negative, damaging comments on her site, along with the circumstantial evidence tracing them back to the company's email server. Kerry explained Charlie's connection to the founder of the obscure browser called Bark.

"Mr. Chapman, you can bet not many people here use that browser to access the Internet or LifeStyleXer email accounts," she pointed out, handing him her cellphone. "Here's a picture taken of them huddled over Charlie's laptop in the cafeteria less than ten minutes ago. Since both the complimentary posts Charlie made—as well as the derogatory comments I *think* he and Beverly conspired together to make—used Bark to access the Internet, we can check the time codes on this picture of Beverly and Charlie and compare it to the time codes of the latest nasty-grams sent ten minutes ago and see if they match up. It's *got* to be them!"

Kerry could tell LifeStyleXer's CEO had begun to do a slow burn.

"This pre-IPO period is a highly sensitive time. If it got out that company insiders were sabotaging your success as one of our most popular bloggers, the media blow-back could possibly diminish our chances for having a successful public offering—to say nothing of damaging you professionally and financially."

Kerry merely nodded, wondering what he would—or could—do about it. Chapman once again flipped through the pages that Tony's team of techies had provided.

"Isn't this at least some sort of professional malfeasance?" she asked. "I agree…it would be terrible if your board or the public knew that one of your vice presidents was doing something like this."

"What I don't understand is why would two of our own employees stoop to this?"

The previous, sleepless night, Kerry had closely compared her previous contract with her revised version Chapman had approved.

"My new contract with you merely changed the terms of *my* service, but all other paragraphs regarding Charlie's redefined deal remained the same, *except* for the fact Charlie was to assume responsibility for managing the team of bloggers you plan to hire." She gave a shrug. "I hate to say it, Mr. Chapman…but keeping track of ten bloggers, their twice-daily posts, and the paperwork involved in shepherding and paying so many independent contractors was going to be a lot of *work*—and from my experience, actual daily assignments are not for our Charlie Boy. I think he was totally pissed off that I renegotiated my deal and he got stuck with more work than he bargained for…and I think wanted to punish me." She hesitated and then added, "And since my contract still says if my supervisor—who, right now, is Beverly Silverstein—doesn't find my work up to par, I can be fired at any time." She pointed to herself. "I was the old girlfriend, so why *wouldn't* Charlie's *new* girlfriend want to be in on this, too?"

It was plain from the scowl on Harry Chapman's face that he agreed that the circumstantial evidence against the two was convincing. "Neither Ms. Silverstein nor Mr. Miller apparently bothered to consider that hurting the CookChic blog could impact the overall health of our company," he fumed.

"So what happens next?"

"Well, I won't even ask how you came by these persuasive printouts, Ms. Hannigan, but the deal between you and me still stands. I will order the site administrator to remove immediately all spurious comments from your blog site credited to our server and the Bark server. We'll post a disclosure that those entries were bogus and apologize to you publicly. As long as you keep up your fine work, I'm certain that you'll meet the requirements of our recent arrangement."

"And what about Charlie and—?"

"They're history." He gathered the paper evidence into a neat stack. "HR will let them know they have to be out of the building within the hour."

"But even if you fire them," Kerry protested, "they can still try more dirty cyber tricks from outside the company if they have the right tech connections."

The CEO slowly shook his head.

"I think that reminding them I will *personally* set up an electronic watch system over your blog from here on out will greatly discourage them from making any more mischief for the rest of their miserable lives!"

"I hope so," Kerry replied, doubtfully.

Harry Chapman chuckled. "I'll also tell them that one more wrong move might open them to federal prosecution for playing nasty little games like this on the World Wide Web. Maybe they'll believe it."

Ren and Kerry—with Tony due to arrive after his shift at the cafeteria—returned to the ranch later than they'd hoped, by which time Jeremy looked as if he were about to keel over.

"Rest right there!" Ren commanded, pointing to the leather couch.

Kerry apologized for their tardy arrival, especially considering the fact that the beauty products contingent was due in less than an hour.

"Jeremy, you've done the lion's share of the prep, so why don't you just supervise from right there and tell me what to do next," she urged.

The chef nodded gratefully and stretched out, sipping water with a slice of lemon floating in it. After a half hour, he admitted he still wasn't feeling particularly well, and Ren insisted he retire to his room.

Between those assembled in the kitchen, including the faithful José, along with Tony Perez, the four worked together as a well-coordinated team. Fortunately, the visitors were fifteen minutes late in arriving and Kerry was relieved that the spread of tapas-like hors d'oeuvres—where every dish made use of Montisi olive oil in some fashion—was both simple to make and a tremendous success. Ren served both as wait staff and the gracious host, insisting that Kerry accompany him to receive kudos from their guests.

After the group had departed for their dinner in Healdsburg, Tony returned to the city and José tackled the few cleanup chores left. Ren untied Kerry's chef's apron from behind her back and hung it on a hook next to several others. He took her by the hand and opened the screen door, leading her into the chilly December air, his arm firmly slung around her shoulders as they made their way up the slope to her cottage.

When they reached the front step, Ren turned and pulled her hard against him. The temperatures were dropping and Kerry burrowed into his chest.

"Mmmm…you feel wonderful," she murmured.

Ren's arms tightened around her. "I like this: pleasure *and* business! You'll be pleased to know that the president of the Organic Cosmetic and Beauty Products Association was intrigued by what he saw here and our idea to make a line of olive oil and lavender based soap, and so forth. In fact, he told me tonight that he'd make introductions, once we have our prototype products ready."

"That's wonderful…" Kerry murmured, reveling in the feel of Ren's chin resting on the top of her head. She heard him chuckle.

"All day long, I couldn't get the vision out of my mind of you in a bathtub full of Montisi lavender bubble bath." He began to kiss a path from her ear down to her neck, whispering, "When we make some of this stuff, I hope you'll let me rub—"

Kerry glanced at her right hand, her palms flat against Ren's chest. The ring's stone glowed like a strong and steady beacon. Then she wrapped her arms around Ren's torso and snuggled, again, against his shoulder. An amazing sense of the *rightness* in every single aspect of her life settled over her.

Ren seized her hands from behind his back.

"Let's go inside or the staff will be gossiping, big time, if they see us making out like this on your front porch."

"Oh, I expect it's far too late to worry about that."

He turned and opened the front door, pulling her gently inside. "Even so…this is better," he said, replacing her arms where they'd been around his waist.

"Oh, yes…"

The cottage's front room was in shadow, with the drapes only half open and to Kerry, it felt as if they were wrapped in their own private cocoon. His hands roamed her back, pressing the length of her body against his, offering clear evidence of his rising ardor. Then he bent down and seized her lips as Kerry felt her ring finger begin to throb, along with other parts of her anatomy.

Yet, in the far recesses of her mind, a familiar fear began to edge into her consciousness as Ren's kisses traced a delicate path down her neck. How could the miracle that had happened to her in the space of a week possibly be *real?* And how could she trust her own judgment after making such a terrible mistake with Charlie? She waited for her own thoughts to caution her against the direction she knew these embraces would lead if she truly allowed her heart to have its way.

But instead, all she heard resounding in her head were five whispered words.

Yes…this is *the one!*

Relief and a sense of utter peace enveloped her as real and reassuring as the warmth of Ren's body next to hers.

Kerry raised her arms to thread her fingers through his hair, a rich, dark gold in the rays of the porch light filtering through the cottage window. Then she leaned back in his arms.

"I can't wait for you to meet my godmother, Angelica Fabrini Doyle. Do you think we have the budget to fly back to New York for Christmas?"

"Well, I already like the sound of her Irish-Italian name. Let me take it up with the Finance Committee." He paused. "Great! They said 'yes.' Economy class."

"She's going to be just wild about you, *Signor* Montisi."

Ren pulled her close again.

"Ah…Kerry Hannigan," he murmured. "You're magic…*this is* magic…"

Kerry smiled against his seeking lips.

"Faith and Begorrah, I do believe it *is*…"

It suddenly occurred to Kerry that it was just past midnight. Today marked a week since Angelica had bestowed on her the heart-shaped gemstone, held between two metal hands and framed by its tiny gold crown. In just a few more hours it would be seven full days since she had placed it on her finger, which meant that soon, the Claddagh would be nothing more than a pretty piece of jewelry…but no matter. Her godmother's gift had worked its enchantment.

And then, the sounds in Kerry's world were that of a breeze blowing gently through the olive trees on the hills that surrounded the cottage. The sage-colored leaves and dormant stalks of lavender sighed in the wind, an echo of other soft exclamations of pleasure and delight.

In the morning following the first night Ren stayed with her in the cottage, Kerry pointed to the Claddagh ring and explained its symbolism: friendship, loyalty and love.

"My godmother gave this to me the day before I moved to California and urged me to know my own heart, just as the inscription says." She slipped off the ring and pointed to the words incised in the metal. "I honestly believe that accepting its message led me to you…but I want to earn my way at the ranch as *myself*, and by my own contributions and talents—and not as your girlfriend."

She searched Ren's face for his reaction as she restored the ring to her finger. He lay stretched out beside her on the bed, one hand cradling his head his head.

"You're not my girlfriend. Didn't you just become my fiancée about an hour ago?"

"That's why I want to wait a year to make our engagement official. Just know, though, that the Claddagh ring will always symbolize what we have together."

She wasn't quite ready to tell him of the still, small voice that she was certain had come from the emerald heart during that first week. Ren seized her hand and admired the ring before replying with the grin that had won her heart from the first.

"I totally understand your wanting to prove yourself here, but trust me," he teased. "We're not fooling anyone."

"Maybe so," she'd replied, "but I like the idea of being secretly engaged. One day, if the ranch is in the black, I'll let you buy me another ring…or I'll take off the Claddagh now, and we can use it as our engagement ring then, if our budget is still tight."

Ren smiled at her with a tenderness that brought tears to her eyes.

"I love that ring," he assured her. "Keep it on, but turn the heart toward your own so it tells the world you've made your choice."

Kerry promptly did as instructed. Ren held her right hand in his.

"Every time we look at it during the year," he said, "we'll *both* know what it means." He kissed her on her nose in quick succession to emphasize each word. "Friendship, loyalty…and love." Then he kissed her properly, murmuring, "Especially, love. Now, come over here, will you please?" he said gruffly, pulling her near.

And so it was—a year to the very day of their first meeting—that Kerry Hannigan and Renato Montisi walked out of Tiffany's in downtown San Francisco one December afternoon. Ms. Hannigan had a brand new square-cut diamond surrounded by small, evenly-sized emeralds on the ring finger of her left hand. In the store, she had slipped the Claddagh into its burgundy leather box and stowed it in her purse with the intention of telling Ren, later this glorious day, how the Ring of Truth had worked magic in their lives.

They were due to pay a visit to Ren's grandmother at the San Francisco Towers, not only to announce their official engagement, but to report on the success of their beauty products line based on the year's olive oil and lavender harvests.

"The fact we didn't lose money the first year is amazing," Ren declared as he parked the car in the garage beneath the Civic Center, "to say nothing of making a modest profit, thanks to all the other things we're doing at the ranch."

"And then you blew most of it on this ring," Kerry said, admiring her left hand for the thousandth time as she got out of the car.

"The last of my VC money," he admitted, "which I am only to happy to spend on the woman I love." Then, he very carefully leaned her against the Mercedes and kissed her senseless.

Before visiting Concetta after her evening meal, they had decided to have an early supper themselves at five o'clock at one of their favorite spots in Opera Plaza, across from San Francisco's magnificent, gold-domed City Hall. Afterwards, Ren proposed a stroll along Van Ness to admire the opera house itself, along with the Herbst Theater, home of the San Francisco Ballet.

They had just finished sharing a salad and a shepherd's pie when Kerry pointed out a noisy group wearing heavy stage makeup entering Max's and crowding into a large booth across from theirs.

"Looks like they're from the opera or ballet," Ren noted. "Probably grabbing a bite after the matinee."

One young woman, Kerry noticed, was silent among her boisterous companions. Her lovely features grew grave, and then tears suddenly began to spill down her heavily painted face. A soft sob escaped her lips and she swiftly rose from her seat at the end of the banquette and dashed outside into the Plaza while her compatriots continued their chatter, oblivious to her distress.

Just then, a waiter appeared, handing Ren their check. Meanwhile, Kerry couldn't take her eyes off the arresting young woman with darkish blond hair and high cheekbones. She was now standing a few feet from their table, but on the other side of the window. Her shoulders began to heave and soon she brought her two hands to cover her face in an expression of anguish that Kerry found difficult to watch. The contrast between the joy that she had been feeling all afternoon, and the abject misery radiating through the pane glass separating the two women, spurred her to action.

"Ren…I'll be right back!"

Her fiancé looked up from signing the credit card slip and his brows furrowed.

"Are you all right?"

"I'm fine," she assured him, jumping up from their booth. "Give me a minute, will you? I'll meet you here in just a sec."

Before Ren could answer, Kerry disappeared from his view and bolted out the front of the restaurant. Digging into her handbag, she wrapped her fingers around the small ring box and walked hurriedly toward the woman laid low by such sorrow.

"Look," she said, breathlessly, "I know you don't know me. I am so sorry for whatever has happened…"

The woman's expression of surprise became one of acute embarrassment and she turned her back on the intruder.

"This may seem kind of crazy," Kerry said in a rush, "but I want you to have something that's very precious to me." She circled the woman and reached for her hand. "Please take this," she urged and thrust the ring box into her palm. "When you feel a bit calmer, take out the ring and read its inscription. There are instructions that came with it when my godmother gave it to me a year ago at a time I was feeling pretty much the way I imagine you feel right now."

The woman stared at Kerry as if she were insane, but lowered her gaze to the well-worn leather ring box. Kerry retrieved the box once again and opened its lid to reveal the ring's gold hands clasping the heart-shaped emerald, topped by its small, golden crown.

"It's called a Claddagh ring," Kerry said explained. "It came from Ireland. It survived the nine-eleven tragedy in New York and who knows what else? I don't totally understand it either, but *read* the instructions folded into the top of the box," she urged, closing the lid and handing it back. "You'll just have to trust me when I say this ring could change your life."

Just then, Ren emerged from the restaurant's front door with a worried expression that brightened as soon as he caught sight of Kerry.

"*There* you are," he called to her. "I thought you'd vanished into thin air."

Kerry turned to the stranger. "Keep the faith that all will be well," she urged softly, and then walked the fifty feet to Ren's side.

As she hooked her arm in his, he asked curiously, "Do you know that woman? She looks absolutely stricken. What's wrong?"

"I could see through the window that she was terribly upset about something, so I ran out to see if I could help."

Ren inclined his head over his shoulder and asked, "Did you find out what had happened?"

Kerry gave a slight shrug.

"Actually, I have no idea…I just wished her a bit of Irish luck, trusting that eventually, everything will be just fine."

Author's Note from Ciji Ware

My first thank-you goes to the two other authors in the anthology *Ring of Truth* in which "The Ring of Kerry Hannigan" first appeared in 2014: Diana Dempsey and Kate Moore. It was an honor to have been a part of that literary effort.

In researching and writing this novella, I owe thanks, too, to talented San Francisco chef, Clare Molla, for sharing her world with me at local food events and over a few terrific lunches.

My gratitude also goes to my treasured friend of longstanding from our KABC Radio days, two-time James Beard awardee and author of the elegant *Seriously Simple* series of cookbooks, Diane Worthington—the person I regularly consult on all things culinary.

My imagining of the magnificent Montisi Olive Ranch was due in large part to the kindness and generosity of McEvoy Ranch manager, Dick Neilsen—recently retired—and his wife Linda who hosted me numerous times among the spectacular olive groves and lavender fields of Petaluma, California.

Deep appreciation is due the Bradley family, owners of Amphora Nueva Berkeley Olive Oil Works, as well as to photographer Anthony Dunn www.adunnphotography.com whose body of work, as well as the beautiful image of the California olive grove on the cover of this book, were truly inspiring.

The wonderful Harry Chapman has my thanks for lending me his name as the CEO in this work.

I also owe a huge debt to the "Ciji Betas" Diane Barr, Cynthia Mason, Linda Hammond, Donna Christie Kolkey, and my sister, Joy Ware—who gave this "draft writer" their early feedback on Version 1.

Pam Headrick of A Thirsty Mind Book Design, formats my manuscripts for Lion's Paw Publishing and is a joy to work with, as is my agent Celeste Fine, of Sterling Lord Literistic, who has no problem with my being a "Hybrid."

Every writer needs a safety net of friendship and support and mine includes Jola Anderson, Janet Chapman, Phoebe Fielding, E.V. Gilbreath, Cheryl Popp, Michael Llewellyn, Tom Rotella, Susan Wintersteen, Cynthia Wright, and Millie Zinman. In addition to the friends just mentioned, the Women's Dog Walking Group makes life in the maritime village where I live a total joy. The "Leader of the Pack" —my wonderful neighbor Carol Hannigan Kavalaris— has often lent me her wisdom and support about things both canine and human.

And finally, gratitude, as always, is due my husband, Tony Cook, my loving partner in life's adventures.

As for my late godmother, Jeanne Cagney, she's with me still…

Ciji Ware
Sausalito, California

About Ciji Ware

In addition to the novella "The Ring of Kerry Hannigan," Ciji Ware is the *New York Times* and *USA Today* bestselling author of eight novels and two nonfiction works. She is the daughter, niece, and descendant of writers (including William Ware, author of the historical romance *Zenobia*, 1896; Henry Ware, author of *On the Formation of the Christian Character*, 1831), so the writing profession is just part of the "Ware family business."

Among her many accolades, she has been honored with the Dorothy Parker Award of Excellence and a *Romantic Times* Award for Best Fictionalized Biography for *Island of the Swans,* and as a result of that book, was made a Fellow of the Society of Antiquaries of Scotland (FSA Scot), a tribute she treasures. In 2012, she was a finalist in the prestigious WILLA (Cather) Literary Award for *A Race to Splendor.*

Ware is also an Emmy-award winning television producer, former radio and TV on-air broadcaster for KABC in Los Angeles, as well as a print and online journalist. As a print reporter, she covered the legendary Karen Silkwood trial in Oklahoma City for *New West* magazine and won an American Bar Association Silver Gavel Award for her story about children of divorce: "Joint Custody: One Way to End The War."

Ware received a BA in History from Harvard University and has the distinction of being the first woman graduate of Harvard College to serve as the President of the Harvard Alumni Association, Worldwide.

When she's not writing, the author loves to cook, "travel for work and see the grandkids in NYC," and is a serious Cavalier King Charles Spaniel fancier. She lives in the San Francisco Bay Area with her husband of thirty-nine years and can be contacted at http://www.cijiware.com.

Titles by Ciji Ware

Historical Novels

Island of the Swans
Wicked Company
A Race to Splendor

"Time-Slip" Historical Novels

A Cottage by the Sea
Midnight on Julia Street
A Light on the Veranda

Contemporary Novels

The Four Seasons Quartet:

That Summer in Cornwall
That Autumn in Edinburgh
That Winter in Venice – coming 2015
That Spring in Paris – coming 2016

Contemporary Novellas

Ring of Truth: "The Ring of Kerry Hannigan"

Nonfiction

Rightsizing Your Life
Joint Custody After Divorce

THE FOUR SEASONS QUARTET:
in print and as an e-book on all online platforms:

THAT WINTER IN VENICE
Available: Fall 2015 in print and e-book on all online platforms.
For Ciji Ware's other titles, visit www.cijiware.com
THAT SPRING IN PARIS: Coming in Spring 2016

19994800R00104

Made in the USA
Middletown, DE
10 May 2015